The Cutting Edge

S.J. Gibbs

ISBN: 9798706934446

DEDICATION

For Fleur

ACKNOWLEDGEMENTS

The author would like to acknowledge the support of her fellow writers and members of JAMS Publishing: Michael Andrews, who did the formatting for publication, and J.M.McKenzie for her valued and continued support. Also AJ Jones who did the proofreading and editing.

She would also like to acknowledge the patience and encouragement of her husband, Steve, and all her family and friends.

CHAPTER 1

At the age of four, Rochelle Erickson's life literally turned upside down, strapped into her car seat in the rear of her parent's car, which was now lying on its roof on the A627(M) motorway, just outside Oldham. She was terrified and disorientated. There was blood everywhere and her Mummy and Daddy weren't answering her screams. They were just lying there, not moving.

A man unbuckled her straps and lifted her out of her seat. He tried to calm her down as he shielded her eyes away from her parents' faces.

"C'mon, my little one. You're okay."

He moved her away from the car as it burst into flames. She watched as some other people dragged her parents out of the fire.

They looked dreadful.

A doctor arrived and took her from the man's arms. He carried her to an ambulance. Blue lights were ablaze everywhere she looked. He was relieved to see that, by some kind of miracle, she had only suffered bruising. He passed her over to a paramedic, who tried to comfort her. He asked her what her name was, but she was drifting in and out of focus and couldn't form the words properly. He reassured her that everything was going to be okay. Her body shook, and her arms and legs thrashed in a violent, uncontrolled frenzy. She had never witnessed anything so frightening in her life.

The hospital seemed huge to Rochelle. A doctor sat her down and talked to her until he was confident she understood that she had been involved in an accident and that her Mummy and Daddy had died.

Everything in the hospital was scary. Rochelle could see through the window. It was dark outside. She was tired, but she couldn't fall asleep. She sat herself up in bed and glanced around the room. There were three other beds with children in them. They all looked as if they were asleep, and there were adults sitting in chairs at the side of their beds. Opposite her, a lady stroked the child's head. Rochelle wanted her own Mummy to come and stroke hers.

"I want my Mummy," she cried.

The lady's smile seemed to dance across her face.

"Where's your Mummy, honey?" she asked.

"My Mummy's gone to heaven." Tears began to form in her eyes, but she fought them back.

A nurse with a kind face came over to Rochelle.

"It's alright, sweetie. It's okay for you to cry, but you're going to be okay. We will look after you here in the hospital until a new home is found for you."

"Can I come home with you?" she pleaded with the nice nurse.

Knowing that Social Services weren't aware of any living relatives, and that there was no sign of any friend of the family who was willing to become her guardian, the nurse brushed the question aside and tried to distract her with some ice cream. But Rochelle didn't want any, as the stuffy air of the hospital ward was making her feel sick.

"Rest your head on this pillow. I'll sit here until you fall asleep, snug and sound." The nurse coughed, covering her wide, thin-lipped mouth with her left hand.

"Can you stroke my hair, like my Mummy does?" Rochelle's eyes darted around the ward.

The nurse fussed over Rochelle, as she stared up at the polystyrene-tiled ceiling. Eventually, her tired eyes closed and she drifted off into a deep sleep.

"There, there, my dear," the nurse said, wiping away a tear from her own eye.

The following day, a lady, called a social worker, introduced herself to Rochelle as Amie. She brought a case packed with some of Rochelle's clothes and toys from her other life, and explained that they would be leaving the hospital and going on a long car journey to a new home, where there would be new children to play and make friends with, and lovely grown-ups to look after her. There wouldn't be a mummy or a daddy, but the grown-ups would do all the things that her parents used to do for her.

Rochelle sat in the back of the car holding Amie's hand as the driver headed towards a city which Amie called Bristol. Amie told her that this was where she was going to live with the other children.

She gripped Amie's hand even tighter. She was petrified.

"How many children will there be? What will it be like?"

"It's a large house, and you'll live there with other children just like you, who can't live with their own families. You'll be looked after by grown-ups who'll care for you, and look after you."

Amie glanced out of the car window at the growing traffic.

They arrived at the large house, and a new lady took her hand and told her to say goodbye to Amie. Tears welled when Amie hugged her and left.

The new lady said, "Hi! I'm Maddie. Come with me and I'll take you to your bedroom."

Maddie took her hand and led her up a long, corridor with lots of huge doors along either side. Maddie opened one of the doors, and they entered Rochelle's new bedroom.

"Now, let's unpack this case, shall we?" Maddie said.

Rochelle's nose itched, "This room smells like our bathroom at home, after my Mummy has cleaned it."

She jumped on the bed. "My Mummy cuddles me at night and reads me bedtime stories."

Glancing upwards, the harsh strip light caused her to blink.

"At home, on my bedroom ceiling, I have twinkle stars."

There was a big, loud, ticking clock on the wall, which she thought was pointless because her Mummy hadn't taught her to tell the time yet, although she could recognise the numbers.

Spotting Fluffy, her kangaroo, being unpacked from the case, she rushed over and snatched him from the lady. She hugged him to her chest. "Fluffy, I'm so glad you haven't gone to Heaven with Mummy and Daddy."

Her eyes fell on a bookshelf, loaded with books.

"Ooh, books! I love books. Can you read me a bedtime story, please?"

She ran her fingers along the bookshelf and then over the spines of the books.

Maddie smiled, "Of course I can. I'm going to be your key worker, which means you are going to be my special little girl. What a pretty little girl you are - such beautiful, big blue eyes."

She took out a gilt photo frame with an old photograph of her Mummy and Daddy in it, and placed it on the bedside table. "There! We will put that right beside your bed, so you can see your Mummy and Daddy whenever you want to."

Rochelle looked at the photograph. Fresh tears plummeted down her cheeks. "Why have they left me? Why have they gone to that stupid place called Heaven? Why didn't they take me with them?"

She wiped her arm across her face to dry her tears. She stared at the flowery curtains and then at the carpet, which had black and white zigzags all over it. They didn't match, everything in her bedroom at home matched because everything was pink.

CHAPTER 2

Maddie picked up the hairbrush from the case and walked towards Rochelle.

"Come here! Let me brush your beautiful hair," she cooed.

Rochelle couldn't think of anything worse. She hated it when her Mummy brushed her hair, and now this lady called Maddie, who she didn't even know, wanted to brush it as well.

Maddie came closer. But Rochelle, with a look of terror in her eyes, launched at her and knocked the black brush flying from her hand.

Picking it up from where it had landed, Maddie whispered, "Maybe we'll just leave it till tomorrow. You must be tired. Let me help you into your pyjamas."

"I'm sorry," Rochelle cried. "I didn't mean

to do it. I don't like my hair being brushed." She stared at the photograph of her Mummy and Daddy.

"It's okay, little one. Let's get you into these pyjamas, and then I'll tuck you into bed. Maybe you could choose a book from the bookshelf, and I could read you a bedtime story?"

Maddie sighed as she read the title of the book Rochelle had selected. It was called, 'With My Mummy'. This was going to be a difficult read., She knew the little board book well. Each page depicted a different Mummy and child enjoying simple fun together.

She watched Rochelle's reaction with relief as she turned to the first page, where the Mummy was zooming around a variety of shops.

Rochelle smiled up at her. "My Mummy and I do that. It's great fun."

Stroking Rochelle's hair back away from her eyes, Maddie continued to turn the pages of the book as she watched the little girl's head sink into the pillow and she began to fall asleep with a faint smile on her pretty face. Maddie tiptoed across the room, turned off the light and closed the door behind her.

In the middle of the night, Rochelle woke up screaming. She had seen her Mummy and Daddy with blood all over their faces, their arms outstretched towards her, but her body wouldn't move towards them.

Sitting upright in the bed, she screamed some more. Everything was dark and she couldn't work out where she was. She heard a door open and the room flooded with light as a lady she didn't recognise flicked on the light switch. The memories came rushing back. This was her new home, but where was Maddie and who was this new lady?

"Hi, Rochelle. I'm Barbara. I'm going to be looking after you at night time. Why are you making all this noise? Did you have a bad dream?"

Barbara sat on the side of her bed, "Would you like a cuddle, sweetheart? You're so little to be here. Didn't Maddie leave you a nightlight? Perhaps she forgot. I'll try and find one for you."

"I want my Mummy and Daddy. They had blood all over their faces."

"I know, sweetheart, but they can't come here. Remember you were told that they've gone to Heaven. Stay here, and I'll go and find you a nightlight."

"Can you leave the big light on? I don't want to see their faces again, not with all the blood on them."

"Of course, sweetheart. I won't be gone long. I'll come straight back once I've found one." In her eagerness not to leave Rochelle on her own for too long, Barbara hurried quickly out of the room.

Rochelle pulled the duvet up over her chin. Her hands were trembling. The clock on the wall was still making the loud ticking noise. If only she could tell the time. Then, she would know when Barbara was coming back. She didn't like being on her own.

It felt like forever before she heard the door open again. Barbara came in with a nightlight in her hand.

"Here, sweetheart," she said. "I've found one. Let's plug it in. It's a penguin. Do you like penguins?"

"Yeah! I went to the zoo with Mummy and Daddy, and we saw some little, blue penguins. They were so funny."

"Well, how wonderful! You can remember that happy time whenever he's switched on, and he will keep you company at night. Oh, and who's this you're cuddling. Is it a kangaroo?"

"Yeah! He's called Fluffy. I'm so glad he's here with me, and not gone to Heaven with Mummy and Daddy."

Barbara gave her a cuddle. "You're safe now, honey. No harm is going to come to you here. But I know how scary it is in the dark. At least, you have some light now."

Barbara sat with her until her eyes closed once more and she had drifted back to sleep. She then left the room without a sound.

Rochelle woke early. "Hello, Fluffy. Hello, Penguin," she said.

She climbed out of bed and looked at the closed door. Was she allowed to go outside of her room? She had used a bathroom somewhere out there last night. Maddie had taken her to it, but she couldn't remember where it was. She put on her pink slippers and crept over to the door. She opened it a few inches and peered through the gap. Nobody was about.

Venturing out into the corridor that she'd walked along when she'd arrived, it seemed longer than she remembered, and she noticed that everything was painted white. She counted the doors as she passed them: five in total. She guessed the other children slept in those rooms. The corridor opened into a kitchen area, which was much bigger than the one at home. The night lady, Barbara, was sitting on one of the stools that were placed around a large table. She was writing in a book.

"Hello, Barbara," she said, cautiously approaching her from behind.

Barbara jumped. "Oh, sweetheart. I didn't hear you creeping up on me. Are you okay? You're awake early. Couldn't you sleep?"

"My Mummy always says I wake up too early when I creep in and jump up and down on her bed in the mornings."

"Well, it's okay to be an early bird here. Would you like some breakfast? Kerrie one of the other little girls, will be awake soon. The other children don't wake up quite so early."

"Mummy and I have a smoothie for breakfast. Can I have one here?" she asked, opening a cupboard door.

"I'm afraid we don't have smoothies, Rochelle. All the other children have their favourite cereals with milk. There's a whole lot of them to choose from. Let me show you."

Looking inside the cupboard that Barbara was holding open for her, she recognised one of the boxes and said, "Cornflakes, please. Mummy makes me those instead of a smoothie sometimes."

She took a stool next to Barbara and was just finishing off her cornflakes when another girl entered the kitchen.

"You're new. Where have you come from? I'm Kerrie. I'm six. How old are you? You look like a baby."

Rochelle stared down into her cereal bowl.

"I'm Rochelle. I'm four, and I'm not a baby."

"Now, now," said Barbara. 'Let's make friends. Of course, Rochelle isn't a baby. She's only a couple of years younger than you are, Kerrie."

"Yeah! Like I said! A baby."

Kerrie poured milk onto her cereals from the big jug that was standing on the table.

Rochelle burst into tears.

"See! Like I said! A baby! And a cry baby at

that."

Kerrie tucked into her breakfast.

Rochelle stopped crying, shivered and then glared sullenly at Kerrie.

"I don't want to be your friend, anyway. I just want my Mummy back."

"Well guess what! None of us has got a Mummy, so you'd better get used to it!"

Rochelle was relieved to see Maddie enter the kitchen.

"Morning, Barbara! Morning, girls! Are we getting along okay?"

"No! We're not! I don't want to be her friend. I want to go back to my room. My tummy and my head hurt."

Rochelle pushed the stool back and darted down the corridor to the safety of her bedroom.

Maddie followed her in. "Once we've washed and dressed you, we can make this room more like your own. Would you like that?"

They hung her clothes in the wardrobe and placed her underwear and jumpers in the chest of drawers. She showed Rochelle three duvet covers and asked her to choose which one she would like to put on her bed. She chose the one with ladybirds on it. Her Mummy liked ladybirds.

Maddie then left the room for a moment, but when she came back, she was carrying a box full of wooden toys.

"These will be your special toys," she said. "You can keep them in here. You won't have to share them with the other children."

As the days turned into weeks and the weeks into months, a routine was established. Bath time, bedtime, mealtimes, chores, play and exercise were all part of her normal daily schedule, and Rochelle began to settle into her new situation. Despite this, she asked the staff the same question every day, "Why did my Mummy and Daddy leave me?"

In September, six months after she had arrived at the children's home, the day came for Rochelle to attend school. Maddie helped her into a pair of maroon tights, a long-sleeved, white shirt and a grey tunic. She helped her to button her maroon cardigan over the top. Rochelle slipped her new, black leather shoes onto her feet and Maddie helped her to buckle them. Rochelle's champagne curls cascaded over her face.

"Stand in front of the long mirror, Rochelle. Look how smart you look," Maddie beamed.

Rochelle ran her moist hands over the coarse material of her dreary, grey tunic. Your Mummy and Daddy would be so proud of you. Now, stand still whilst I brush your hair and tie it into bunches for you."

Maddie stood back to admire how Rochelle looked. She was a pretty little girl, but Maddie reflected how small and vulnerable she looked. She felt sad that Rochelle didn't have one of her parents to take her to school on her first day.

She loaded her onto the school bus along with the other children, and blinked back a tear. She wiped it away before anyone saw it. It wouldn't be professional to show any emotion.

Waving her off on the home's private minibus, she noticed Rochelle's blank expression. She appeared to be staring out of the window, as if oblivious to what was going on around her.

Maddie sighed. She'd been trying her best to make her happy, but Rochelle's temper tantrums had increased over the last couple of months. She was often tired, because her sleeping pattern was still disturbed. She still complained of headaches, but the doctors had said that they would pass. They were a symptom of the trauma of losing her parents.

The first day of school was a disaster for Rochelle. She spent the whole morning in tears. Not only was she missing her Mummy and Daddy, but she was missing Maddie as well now.

Why had Maddie sent her here? She should have stayed at the home like she had every other day that all the other children had gone to this stupid place called school.

The afternoon was even worse. All the other children laughed at her when liquid dripped down her legs and formed a puddle on the classroom floor.

Miss Webster had shouted at her.

"Why on earth didn't you ask to go to the toilet?"

The others had laughed even louder, as she was dragged from the classroom to be changed into some spare, old school clothes.

By the time she was back on the minibus, she had decided she hated school with its stupid rules and troublesome schoolwork. She hated Miss Webster, and she hated the other children.

She didn't like the children's home, but school was even worse.

CHAPTER 3

Rochelle's birthday came and went. She had turned five. There was a cake and candles, and they all sang 'Happy Birthday' to her, but she ran to her room, crying. She wanted her Mummy and Daddy.

The following day, she was sitting on the school bus next to Kerrie, who was now seven, when Kerrie began to tease her. Feeling a growing sense of rage, Rochelle pushed her.

"What did you do that for? Why did you punch me?" Kerrie moved further back into her own seat.

"I didn't punch you. I pushed you."

Again, she pushed Kerrie, right in the centre of her chest. Then she hit her on the arm.

"That's a punch! I suppose you'll go telling tales on me now."

The bus jolted to a stop at a red light. Kerrie sank to the floor and started to cry.

Rochelle yanked her by her ear. "Stop it! You'll get me into trouble."

Wiping the tears from her eyes with a trembling hand, Kerrie asked, "Why are you so mean? None of the other children are as mean as you."

Later, during the long, tedious week, Rochelle decided that she was going to yell, "NO!", every time anyone spoke to her or asked her to do anything. She threw things and slammed doors, in the desperate hope that they'd become so annoyed with her, they would go and find her Mummy and Daddy and bring them back from Heaven.

Maddie made her a star chart and stuck it onto Rochelle's bedroom door. If she behaved herself, she would get a silver star. When she'd got five stars, she would get a treat.

"How many stars do I need to get to be able to see my Mummy?" she asked.

"I've explained to you, sweetheart, your Mummy is in Heaven with your Daddy. You can't see them yet, but if you look up to the sky, where the planets, stars and galaxies of the universe are, you might see Heaven. It's a beautiful place where angels sit on clouds playing harps."

She pointed upwards through the bedroom window.

"I don't care about the stupid silver stars on your chart," Rochelle replied.

Things became even worse for Rochelle, when Maddie told her she was leaving the care home and another lady was to become her key worker. Rochelle's response was a deafening silence.

The new lady was named Jeanna, and she was much stricter than Maddie had been. She removed the star chart and explained that she didn't *reward* good behaviour - she *expected* it! She told Rochelle that the reason they hadn't been able to find a new Mummy and Daddy for her to go and live with was because she was too naughty.

Well, she didn't want a new Mummy and Daddy, anyway. She just wanted her own back.

Rochelle watched from the kitchen window, as Kerrie left the children's home holding hands with *her* new Mummy and Daddy. She didn't care, she didn't like Kerrie and the new parents didn't look anything like the ones in the photograph by her bed.

So, she learned that people come and go. Your Mummy and Daddy leave you to go to Heaven. People who look after you, like Maddie, leave to go to other jobs, and children like Kerrie leave to live with new Mummies and Daddies. None of them come back. Once they've gone, you don't see them again.

One day, Rochelle took a pair of scissors from the kitchen drawer and hid them inside her jumper. She had taken a real dislike to one of the new girls because she had heard Jeanna praising her and telling her what gorgeous, dark, shiny hair she had. Well, she would teach her a lesson; she would sneak behind her and cut off the stupid ponytail she insisted on wearing.

This landed her in big trouble.

Jeanna shouted, "Go to your room, you horrible child!"

Rochelle watched as Jeanna removed all of her toys and locked the big, solid bedroom door behind her. "You can stay in here until you're ready to say you're sorry."

Well, Rochelle wasn't sorry. She took out the crayons she'd hidden underneath her mattress, and drew pictures all over her walls. She was in serious trouble with Jeanna afterwards and was made to scrub her artwork off.

Later, as she sat sulking at the dining room table, waiting for her breakfast, Sharna, who had been at the home since Rochelle had arrived, whispered something Rochelle was unable to hear to the girl whose hair she had cut off.

Rochelle flew from her chair and grabbed Sharna by her hair, pulled her off the chair onto the floor, and then kicked her in the head. She gave her one strong punch in the face before she was dragged away by Jeanna and one of the other staff, whose name she couldn't even remember.

Rochelle's sixth birthday came and went with the same result as her fifth: a cake, candles, a 'Happy Birthday' song, tears, and a stropping off to her bedroom.

Jeanna had left and had been replaced by another key worker, named Yvette who was softer and kinder, but she didn't keep as close an eye on Rochelle as the other had, which meant Rochelle's rude behaviour often went unchecked.

CHAPTER 4

Shortly after her birthday, Rochelle was poorly, so she was taken to see the doctor at his surgery. He prescribed her with a course of antibiotics for a chest infection.

During the night, she became boiling hot, and she was dripping with sweat. Her heart was thumping way too fast, and she was struggling to take air into her lungs.

An ambulance was called for her, and Yvette travelled with her, stroking her hair and fussing over her all the way to the hospital. Blood tests were taken, and Rochelle was diagnosed with sepsis.

"Am I going to Heaven to see my Mummy and Daddy?" she asked Yvette, placing her hands in a praying position.

"No! The doctors and nurses are going to

help you get better. The doctors are doing tests, and I'm going to stay here. I'll only leave you after you've gone to sleep, and the doctors and nurses will look after you during the night."

She reached for Yvette's hand.

"I want my Mummy. I hate being in hospital, it reminds me of before."

Yvette stroked her cheek.

"I know, but she can't come, so that's why I'm here."

"It stinks in here! It smells of old people … and poo! Why is that machine beeping? Why is the little girl over there crying? Am I going to die?"

A nurse with a kind voice approached.

"We're going to move you to a special ward now, where you will be able to get some sleep. There will be four children on the ward.

"Maybe once Rochelle's settled, you could go home for a bit, Yvette?"

Yvette smiled.

"Yes. It's been a rough night. I'll see her settled and then go home. I'll head back about lunchtime, if that's okay?"

Rochelle was moved from the accident and emergency department to a ward of four. The other three beds were occupied, but she couldn't see any of the other children's faces. They all appeared to be asleep, but at least it meant she wouldn't be on her own.

After a nurse had put a needle in her hand and had attached a tube to a bag hanging on a metal stand, Yvette kissed her on the cheek and explained that she needed some rest, but would come back to the hospital as soon as she could.

"Be brave, Rochelle. I'll be back soon. I promise."

Rochelle's expressive blue eyes followed Yvette until she was out of sight. She was even more terrified now that she had left, and wished she hadn't been so horrible to her at the home. Maybe, then, she would have stayed. Confused, she drifted off to sleep, her mouth pursed but slightly open and loose.

She woke up startled. Where was she? Nothing was familiar. A needle, attached to a tube, was sticking out of her hand. Her eyes followed the tube to a bag of clear liquid hanging on a metal stand. She screamed.

A woman in a white dress, who she didn't recognise, came over.

"It's okay, come on let's tuck you back under these sheets."

"Where am I? Where's Yvette? What's this in my hand?"

She pulled at the tube.

"It's okay. You're in hospital. I'm the nurse looking after you. Yvette will be back soon.

"You've been asleep, and you've forgotten where you are, that's all. The needle in your hand is giving you the medicine you need to help make you better."

Rochelle sobbed.

"I don't want Yvette to come back. I want my Mummy. Why is my heart thumping so fast?"

She glared at the bleeping machine at the side of the bed.

CHAPTER 5

After a six-week stay in hospital, Rochelle returned to the home. She was still too poorly to attend school as she was still tired, weak, suffering from chest pain and her joints were still swollen.

Her teacher was sending schoolwork to the home, but no one was available to help her with it. She spent most of her days in her bedroom, either sleeping or daydreaming. She no longer had a key worker, as Yvette had left even before Rochelle had been discharged from the hospital, and no one had replaced her.

It wasn't so bad for her during the day, when the others were at school, but she dreaded the evenings and weekends, when one girl, Sharron, who was nine, had spotted her weakness and had started to bully her whenever she saw an opportunity. Being two years older than Rochelle, she had the clear advantage of size.

The children's home had fallen into an untidy, dreary mess due to a major shortage of trained staff and inconsistent management. Therefore, the general supervision of the children was poor and inadequate.

One Saturday morning over breakfast in the kitchen, not long after Rochelle's seventh birthday, Sharron declared to the other four girls that they were not to speak to Rochelle.

"She's a vile, weak creature and none of you are to speak to her ever again. Do you all understand?"

With no staff within earshot, the other four girls agreed to the cruel plan. They were all scared of Sharron and were prepared to go along with whatever she told them to do.

As a result, Rochelle shut herself off in her bedroom whenever she could. The skeleton staff were happy with this situation as it left them one less problem to deal with. A child who was introverted, quiet and reclusive made their lives much easier.

At this vulnerable point in her life, Rochelle

dreamed about what it would be like to live with new parents. She was miserable at the children's home with no key worker and no friends. She was even missing going to stupid school.

Around this time, she developed an enthusiasm for reading. Selecting a book from the far left of the extensive bookshelf in her bedroom, her aim was to read every single book available to her.

As her world grew through the books she devoured, her confidence, self-esteem and self-awareness blossomed. On her return to school, her mind was sharp. She was now literate and proved herself to be a quick learner.

As her eighth birthday approached, Janet filled the empty key worker position for Rochelle. She warmed to the young girl straight away, and with her own love of books and reading, was able to establish an immediate rapport.

"Why have you never been placed with a family?" she asked Rochelle.

"Because I'm too naughty. But I don't think I'm as bad as I was when I first came here. I missed my Mummy so much then. Now, I struggle to remember her. I have to look at her photograph to remind me what she looked like. It would be nice to live with new parents."

With a sigh, she closed the book she'd been reading and turned her head to look straight at Janet.

"Can you help me find a new family?" she asked.

"I can try. I'll bring your case forward at the next review meeting. You deserve to have some love in your life. You're such a sweetie."

In bed that night, Rochelle fell asleep feeling happier than she'd done since the day her parents had been killed.

A new family! New parents! Maybe it wouldn't be so bad.

CHAPTER 6

Sure enough, Janet kept her word, and before long, Rochelle was at the top of the list for recommendation for adoption. Finally, she had a chance to leave the home.

"Stand still, Rochelle, and let me plait your hair! Are you excited about going for lunch with your prospective new parents?" Janet asked.

"Yes. I like them. They seem nice. But I'm a bit scared about being on my own with them for the first time. It's always been safe when you've been there with us. I'm excited to be going to a restaurant for lunch, though. I hope I don't spill anything down my new dress. It was kind of them to have bought it for me. Should I call them Mummy and Daddy or stick with Derek and Gloria?"

"I'd stick with Derek and Gloria for now."

The doorbell of the home rang, and Rochelle rushed to her window.

"They're here! I wasn't sure they'd come."

Janet escorted Rochelle to the front door, where Derek and Gloria were waiting. Her new Mummy and Daddy! It was scary, but also very exciting.

"Oh, my love! You look so pretty," declared Gloria. "The dress suits you. I knew the green one would look good on you."

She leaned over and patted Rochelle's head.

"Yes! Thank you, Gloria. I love it."

Derek smiled his kind smile at Rochelle, which made her feel special. They were such nice people; she would be so lucky if they decided to allow her to go and live with them.

As they drove to the restaurant, she daydreamed about what her new life would be like. She would have to remember to be well-mannered and polite during lunch, to make them want to take her home with them.

The lunch went well, and she remembered

to speak in the correct manner, dotting in a 'please' and a 'thank you' as often as possible. She smiled a lot and was cheery, but this wasn't an act; she was happy. They seemed to like her, but first and foremost, she liked them.

The next few short visits went well, and it was only a couple of months later that she was packed and sitting on the end of her bed anxiously waiting for her new Mummy and Daddy to collect her and take her to her new forever home. Her brain was galloping in every direction as to what it may be like.

Safely belted into the PT Cruiser, with all of her belongings packed carefully in the boot, she was excited to begin the journey to her new life. Spreading out in the back of the car, she was pleased they didn't have any other children. That meant she wouldn't have to share them.

"It's a long way to Windermere," Derek explained. "It'll take us about four and a half hours to get there, but we'll stop somewhere nice for a bite of lunch to break the journey."

"Tell me about Windermere. I'm so excited to see my new home."

Rochelle wriggled in the back seat of the car.

"We've told you a bit about it already," Gloria piped up. "It's a delightful place: a small town, much smaller than Bristol, which is a city. It's about a mile from the largest lake in England. There are shops, a splendid library and a railway station. It has fantastic views of the lake and the peaceful, open countryside. There's a large hotel, guesthouses, and coffee shops. Orrest Head lies opposite the station and people come from all over the world to walk in the craggy fells. You're going to love it."

"Where will I go to school, and how will I get there?"

"Well, as you already know, Derek is a headmaster, but not at the school you'll be going to. You'll go to the local primary school, and you'll make lots of new friends. I'll be taking and collecting you each day, as I only work part-time in the gift shop in town."

"Tell me about my new home again, please. I love hearing about it. I can't wait to get there. Are we nearly there yet?"

Rochelle fidgeted with her seat belt.

Derek laughed. "No! I told you it's a long journey. Gloria and I have lived there for over 20 years now. The nearest large town is a 30-

minute drive away from our house. Our home is kind-of large, with beautiful gardens. It has four bedrooms and we've decorated one of them especially for you. Yours has its own little walk-in shower room attached. It's called an en-suite. We have our own separate en-suite too, which leads off our bedroom. There's a living room, a dining room, which is quite grand, a sparkling, modern kitchen, and we also have a little semi-circular conservatory and a large downstairs cloakroom with a toilet. Gloria takes great pride in our home, and now it's going to be yours, as well."

Rochelle leant back in the seat and watched as they passed a long row of tall trees, which looked like towers. The sun scorched through the car window. This was the best journey she had ever been on. She couldn't thank them enough for having taken her away from the children's home.

After a short while, she closed her eyes and drifted off into a contented sleep, dreaming of her new home.

"Bless her," Gloria said to Derek. "She's fallen asleep with a little smile on her face. Maybe we should skip lunch if she doesn't wake up."

A short while later, as they approached the driveway, Gloria gave Rochelle a little nudge.

"C'mon! Wake-up, my love! We're here. I can't wait to show you your new home."

Rochelle was out of the car before they'd barely come to a stop.

"My new home! My new home! I love it already. Is this my front garden?"

The sun shone down on Rochelle as she ran around taking it all in. Twirling, with her arms raised high in the air, she breathed in the summer air. The birds sang as if welcoming her. Another sound tinkled, and she ran towards the front porch to investigate where it came from. Fascinated, she tried to reach up to touch the shiny metal thing, which was making this lovely sound.

"What is it?" she shouted. "I've never seen one of these."

"It's a wind chime, darling. Doesn't it make a beautiful sound?"

Gloria had caught her up.

"Oh, we've so much to show you, and to teach you."

"I feel so high up. Look down there at the sea."

Derek turned the key in the front door lock.

"It's not the sea, Rochelle. It's the lake Gloria told you about earlier. Once we've put your belongings in your room, maybe we could all go to the hotel down by the lake and have afternoon tea, seeing as we skipped lunch whilst you were asleep. You must be starving. I know I am."

Rochelle, over-excited, forgot herself and pushed past Derek into the entrance hall. Her new home. She couldn't believe it. She opened the first door on the left. The living room, she presumed. Large, but a bit boring, she thought – all very tidy, no toys or mess, but there was a TV.

There were some glass doors leading off to the conservatory. Wow! The view was amazing. She could see the lake in the distance. She opened the back door, which led on to a patio area with an outdoor dining table and chairs. She doubled back on herself and found the dining room again. That looked boring, too, but there was a computer on a desk in the corner. She wondered if she would be allowed to use it.

"Come on, Rochelle," Gloria called from the hallway. "Let's take you upstairs and show you your bedroom."

She ran up the stairs, with Gloria following behind her.

"The door on your left, Rochelle – that's your bedroom. I hope you like it."

Rochelle didn't know what she had expected, but this was not it. She looked around the room and felt disappointed. It was boring, as well. It was too tidy: cream walls with no pictures or clock, light brown furniture, no ornaments, no toys, no bookshelf like she'd had at the home. The only real colour in the whole room was a pink duvet covered in big white circles.

She blinked back a tear. It wouldn't do for her to cry. Gloria and Derek might put her straight back in the car and drive her back to the home. She smiled her brightest smile.

"I love it, Gloria. Thank you."

The hotel by the lake was lovely, and they sat at a table on the lawn, which ran down to the water's edge. The waitress brought out little triangle-shaped sandwiches and scones oozing with clotted cream and strawberry jam. Gloria ordered Rochelle a limeade over ice, which Rochelle had never even heard of before, never mind tasted. It was delicious.

She was unaware that she was tapping her

fingers on the table until Derek snapped, "Stop tapping, Rochelle. We don't do that at the table!"

She glared at him defiantly and carried on tapping.

"I'm not hurting anyone, am I?"

"I won't be spoken to like that, Rochelle. Gloria and I expect certain standards from you. We are offering you a nice life here with us, but there will be rules. They will be different to the ones at the children's home, and you will respect us."

Rochelle stopped tapping and pulled a sulky face. Firstly, her bedroom was boring and now Derek had said she wasn't even to tap her fingers at the table.

Maybe living with Gloria and Derek wasn't going to be such fun after all.

CHAPTER 7

After a restless night in her new bed, Rochelle rose early and ventured downstairs in her dressing gown and slippers.

Derek glanced over the top of his newspaper.

"Morning, Rochelle. Why aren't you washed and dressed? Have you used the shower like Gloria showed you? Go upstairs, and shower and dress, please."

Rolling her eyes, Rochelle headed back upstairs, and once out of his sight, gave him her middle finger. For goodness sake, a shower every morning before she was even allowed downstairs …!

The shower burst into action as she turned the round knob in the way Gloria had shown her when she'd made her take a shower the previous night. She hadn't the slightest intention of getting into it, though. They'd never know.

Taking the top off the unfamiliar toothpaste, she squirted some onto her pink and green toothbrush and held it under the cold water tap until it was all gone. This was a cunning trick she'd learned at the children's home. When they asked if you'd cleaned your teeth and you lied, the wet toothbrush would confirm your story.

While she got dressed, she left the shower to run a little longer in case Derek or Gloria was listening. She wet the hairbrush and brushed her hair with it until it looked wet enough. She turned off the shower after wetting a fluffy, brown towel and throwing it onto the tiled shower room floor.

Pleased with herself, she headed back downstairs. Gloria was singing in the kitchen, so she sneaked past the living room door hoping that Derek would still be reading his newspaper and wouldn't notice her.

"Morning, sweetie. What would you like for breakfast?" Gloria asked.

"I don't eat much for breakfast, only cereals. But when I used to live with my real Mummy and Daddy, they used to make me smoothies. I love them … I think! I can't remember too well. I never had one at the home. Can I make one here?"

"I'll make you a special banana smoothie and you can see if you like it. We can experiment with different fruits to see which one you like best. Your Mummy must have been a very special lady."

"I'm beginning to forget her … my Daddy too. Thank you for putting their photo by my bed. I kiss them goodnight, every night. But, unless I look at the photo, I struggle to remember their faces now."

Gloria blended the bananas with some milk and passed the smoothie over to Rochelle. It was yummy.

"You can talk to me whenever you want to about your real Mummy and Daddy, you know. You must never forget them. I'm sure they loved you very much.

"Now, because it's school holidays, Derek will be at home, and I've taken the next four weeks off work too, so we can all get to know each other. This morning, you and I have a hair appointment at the hairdressers in town. We need to get you looking shipshape. You've got beautiful hair, but it needs a good cut. Did you wash your hair with shampoo this morning, like I showed you last night … only it looks a little bit lank and greasy?"

The lie fell off Rochelle's tongue.

"Oh, yes, Gloria. The shampoo smelt delightful."

"Great! Now, in the mornings, Derek likes to read his paper in peace, so I suggest you go and choose a book to read. There are plenty to choose from in the cupboard in the hallway. Derek and I have taken great pleasure in choosing an assortment for you. I hope you like them."

"Oh! I didn't know there were books in the house. I love reading."

Rochelle ventured into the plain, beige-coloured hallway and found the cupboard that Gloria had referred to. Inside, it was huge; her head didn't even touch the ceiling. She switched on the light and almost cried with joy when she saw that it was like a small library, with shelf after shelf full of books. Derek and Gloria must read a lot. Her eyes widened when she spotted her name on the ledge of one of the shelves … 'Rochelle's Books'. She squealed with delight as she ran her fingers across the spines. There were so many titles that she hadn't yet read, and lots she hadn't even heard of before. She chose 'The Great Fire Dogs' by Megan Rix.

Overwhelmed and excited, she ran into the living room and flung herself at Derek, giving him a huge hug.

"Oh, Derek! Thank you so much. You don't know how happy you've made me. I love books, and now I have loads of them ... and even a shelf with my name on it."

Derek eased her away from him.

"I didn't expect that strong a reaction from you. You'll fit in well here if you enjoy books. Which one have you chosen?"

She showed him the one she'd selected.

"I've already read two of her books: 'Emmeline and the Plucky Pup' and 'The Bomber Dog'. This one's about two dogs, and what happened to them during The Great Fire of London."

Derek lifted his newspaper.

"That's wonderful. Now choose a place to sit and enjoy your book."

Rochelle headed into the conservatory, curled herself into a chair and opened her book at the first page. She stared out at the view of the lake for a few moments and then read the first line.

After what seemed like only five minutes to Rochelle but was actually an hour, she heard Gloria calling her name.

"Rochelle, get your red jacket. We need to leave now to get to the hairdressers on time."

"Do we have to? I'd rather stay here and read. I'm getting to a good point in the story."

Gloria laughed.

"Come on! You can bring your book with you. Hurry up, else we'll be late."

As Rochelle sat in the big black chair looking at herself in the mirror, the hairdresser asked her what hairstyle she would like. She tilted her head to one side. Nobody had ever asked her such a question. In fact, she had never even been inside a hairdresser's shop before.

"I don't know."

She looked at Gloria's reflection in the mirror for guidance.

"Well, I presume you will want to keep the

length, but it's so scraggly. It needs a good tidy-up," the hairdresser continued.

Gloria stood behind her watching closely whilst the hairdresser chopped away at Rochelle's hair.

Rochelle read her book. She was so engrossed in the story that she didn't notice the hairdresser stop at one point and have a whispered conversation with Gloria.

As they left the salon, Gloria began to scratch her head.

"Lice, Rochelle! You've got head lice! Didn't they wash your hair at the home?"

"Lice! What do you mean, Gloria? I don't know what lice is? What *is* lice?"

"They're horrible little creatures that live in dirty girls' hair. I'm so embarrassed. We'll have to go to the chemist and ask them what we can use to get rid of them."

The walk home was a quiet one. Obviously the lice thing had really distressed Gloria. She looked as though she was in shock.

As they entered the hallway back at home, Gloria shouted, "Derek, she's got head lice. I've never been so embarrassed in all my life."

Derek laughed.

"Oh, Gloria! Don't be so dramatic. All kids get head lice. My school's full of them. I'm forever having to write to parents to inform them we've had yet another outbreak. Did you get her a treatment from the chemist?"

"Yes, of course!" Gloria sighed, ushering Rochelle upstairs, medical treatment in her trembling hand.

She took out the leaflet from the box and read the step-by-step instructions. Rochelle sat on her bed crying as the foul-smelling treatment was applied.

"I'm sorry, Gloria. I didn't know you got the horrid lice thing from not washing your hair. I'm sorry. I didn't wash my hair this morning. I lied. I'm so sorry. I won't do it again."

"Oh, Rochelle! You didn't get head lice from not washing your hair this morning. You caught them at the children's home. It'll be fine. The treatment will get rid of them.

"You're naughty to have lied, though. We'll have no more lies, please. I won't tell Derek this time, but if I catch you lying again, I *will* tell him and there will be consequences."

'Consequences'! Rochelle hadn't heard the word before. It wasn't in any of the books she had read. What did it mean? She scratched her head, horrified at the thought of horrid little creatures crawling around in her hair.

Rochelle had to keep the treatment on her hair until the following morning, when it could be washed off. Gloria had explained that they would need to use the fine-toothed, nit comb to remove the dead lice. She had used the weighty word 'consequence' again when she'd explained that, as a *consequence* of the treatment, they wouldn't be able to leave the house again until all the lice had been eradicated.

After a lovely salad lunch – Gloria had called it Caesar Salad – they spent the afternoon reading. Rochelle curled into the same chair in the conservatory where she had positioned herself prior to the hairdresser ordeal and read until she'd finished her book. She enjoyed the tranquillity. There were no rowdy children around to disturb her peace. Even the awful smell coming from her hair couldn't permeate her feeling of contentment.

For some reason, as she closed her book, a memory of baking with her Mummy came back to her: the delicious smell of the cakes as they baked inside the oven, the taste of licking the wooden spoon after they'd finished stirring the mixture.

She went into the living room.

"Gloria, could we do some baking together, please? Mummy and I used to bake a lot, and it's one of my happiest memories of her."

Gloria rested her book on the coffee table.

"Of course, we can, my love. What a wonderful idea! Let's get to it straight away, shall we?

"Derek, we're going to bake you a fancy cake," she exclaimed.

Rochelle followed Gloria into the big, well-designed kitchen, where everything had its place.

As they stirred the mixture in the bowl, Rochelle asked, "Will I ever not miss my Mummy and Daddy? I know you are my parents now, but will I ever call you Mum and Dad?"

Gloria smiled at her and offered her the spoon to lick.

"You'll never *not* miss them. They are a part of you. I hope Derek and I will do a good job as your new parents, and you'll learn to love us.

"You know, we've wanted a little girl of our own for such a long time. Your coming into our lives means everything to us. You can call us Mum and Dad if you want to, but it's entirely up to you. We're more than happy if you prefer to call us Gloria and Derek.

" I can't wait to give Derek his cake. How long will it take in the oven?"

Their first family dinner went well. Gloria had cooked them steak, chips and peas, which tasted much nicer than anything Rochelle had ever eaten at the home. After they'd finished, she'd enjoyed the family time around the dining table. She had remembered to be polite, and had made sure she didn't tap her fingers on the table.

She'd also enjoyed chatting after the meal. Derek had asked her all about 'The Great Fire Dogs', which she'd been thrilled to tell him all about. She'd particularly relished having his full attention.

Eventually, Derek pushed his chair back and moved away.

"It's time for you to help Gloria with the dishes now, Rochelle, and when they're done, we will see if we can find something suitable to watch on TV."

"What do you mean help Gloria with the dishes?" Rochelle looked confused.

"To wash up, Rochelle … and clean the kitchen."

"No! I'm coming with you to watch TV in the lounge," she retorted.

Derek raised his voice.

"You will do as you're told, young lady."

"I won't! I'm not cleaning the kitchen. That's your job … to look after me. I want to watch TV."

She began to move towards the lounge.

"Didn't you have to help at the children's home?" Derek asked.

"No! That's what the staff were for. And that's what you're for … Mums and Dads! That's what they do. They do all those jobs. Some type of Dad you are, if you expect me, the child, to do it."

She attempted to move past Derek in the doorway.

"Rochelle, that's enough!" Derek scolded. "Go to your room and don't come out again until you're prepared to say you're sorry for what you've just said."

Rochelle raced to the book cupboard and selected another book, but as she put her foot on the first step, Derek snatched the book from her.

"No books until your behaviour improves!" he snapped.

CHAPTER 8

The day arrived for Rochelle to start school at the local primary, Green Valley. Gloria had made sure she looked smart in her green-striped summer dress, bottle green cardigan, whiter-than-white ankle socks with little frills, and dark brown school shoes. She had even plaited her hair with matching green hair bobbles.

"Put your blazer on to walk to school in, please, Rochelle. You won't need to wear it during the day as the weather is so glorious, but they insist that you wear one outside of school."

Rochelle kicked at the pavement as they walked to her new school. The last few weeks had been turbulent, with lots of highs, but lots of lows as well. She'd tried to behave, but she seemed to be able to upset Derek without doing much at all.

The only child she had met during this period had been a disaster. Gloria had invited her friend over to the house with her daughter, Cara, who was going to be in the same class as her at school. But Rochelle didn't want another child in her new home, so she had become obtrusive, refusing to interact with her. As a result, she had been sent to her room.

As she walked to school, she now wished she'd been kinder to Cara. It would have been nice to have a friend there. She just knew that Cara would have told the other children how mean she was. Nobody would want to speak to her, let alone be her friend.

Gloria kissed her goodbye at the school gates.

"Have a good day. Be kind to the other children, and do what the teacher tells you to. I'll be waiting here at the end of the day for you."

A female teacher stood inside the doorway, holding a clipboard. Unsmilingly, she asked, "What's your name?"

"I'm Rochelle … Rochelle Erickson," she said, looking down at the floor.

The teacher looked at her printed list and placed a tick alongside Rochelle's name.

"You're in Class 5, Rochelle. Welcome to Green Valley. Your classroom is along the short corridor to the left. It has Class 5 written on the door."

Rochelle, looked around her. There seemed to be children everywhere, all dressed in green. All of a sudden, her tummy hurt. She needed the toilet, but where were they? A memory of wetting herself at her previous school came rushing back to her, and in a panic, she ran along the corridor to try and find the toilets.

As she turned the corner at the end, she bumped straight into another teacher, knocking a pile of books from his arms.

"My goodness, child. Where are you off to in such a hurry? We don't allow running inside the school," he scolded.

"I need the toilet. I'm new, and I don't know where they are," she burst out.

The stout teacher smiled at her. He had a kind face.

"It's over there. And walk, don't run." He pointed towards a big, green door to his right that said Girls' Toilets on it.

Opening the cubicle door and locking it behind her, she quickly pulled down her bottle green knickers and sat on the toilet seat, feeling relieved that she'd made it in time. She took longer than she should have done. She didn't want to go to Class 5 and meet her new teacher and all of those children. She knew they wouldn't like her.

She didn't bother washing her hands – there was no one around to see – and dawdled back towards the Class 5 classroom.

"Oh! You're the new girl," she heard the same teacher whose books she'd knocked to the floor say.

"Children, this is Rochelle Erickson, who has come to join our class."

It seemed like a hundred pairs of eyes had fixed their stare on her as she stood in front of the entire class, not knowing what to do.

"Now, who would like to be Rochelle's buddy, and show her around the school today?"

Rochelle scanned the class looking for a potential friend, but she couldn't see any raised hands. Her stomach turned. She hoped she wasn't going to vomit.

The teacher looked a little surprised.

"Okay! I'll choose someone then. Cara, you can be Rochelle's buddy."

Cara rolled her deep, brown eyes as her best friend was moved away from her to another desk to allow Rochelle to sit next to her.

As Rochelle took her seat, Cara whispered, "Great! Now I'm stuck with you."

"Well, I'm not happy about being stuck with you, either!"

Rochelle glared at her and edged further across her seat away from her.

Rochelle's first day was a nightmare. Cara proved to be more enemy than buddy, being spiteful to her and taking every opportunity she could to alienate her from the other children by teasing her into making a fool of herself.

The next few weeks proved to be no better. She got into trouble for daydreaming, forgetting things, and she struggled to pay attention in lessons. She was distracted and unhappy most of the time. At playtimes, she took herself off to a corner of the playground with a book, but this also resulted in the other children ridiculing her for being different from them.

At home, things were a little better. She had enjoyed going to the vast art museum with Derek, and he had been impressed with how interested she had been in what he had explained to her about the art installations and artists. She loved the time she had on her own with Derek, when she had all of his direct attention.

"You're such a clever little girl," Derek said as they left the museum. Rochelle beamed at him. If only it could always be like this.

Another special day had been spent walking with Derek and Gloria. They had taken the east shore footpath from Howtown, along Ullswater, past the reservoir to Glenridding. The walk was easy and pretty. They had stopped at a quaint, little café for lunch, and taken a steamer across the lake, the scenery changing whichever way she looked. She'd seen waterfalls and clear, deep pools, and Derek had promised that, next summer, they would go camping and he would teach her kayaking. He'd also talked to her about farming practices, mining and local history as they'd crossed streams and woods. The sun had shone, and Rochelle's energy and enthusiasm had matched it in equal measures.

Back at school, things were getting worse as she struggled to focus in class. She was frustrated with the other children for not liking her, and her inner rage had been festering towards Cara.

"You're a filthy, scheming bitch, Cara!" Rochelle told her as they headed to the playground, one lunchtime.

"Well, I'm not the one who was spiteful when I came to your house to play. I didn't even want to come to yours. Why would I want to meet some kid whose parents had been killed in a car crash, and who was an orphan?"

Rochelle turned and punched her straight in the face. Blood splattered everywhere. With one punch, she'd broken Cara's nose.

"I'm sorry, I didn't mean to punch you."

Rochelle reached out to help her up from the cold, concrete floor of the playground.

It was dreadful … total pandemonium.

Cara screamed!

Rochelle screamed!

Lots of the other children screamed!

Teachers appeared from everywhere.

Rochelle was sent to the headmistress's office, and Gloria was asked to attend the school urgently.

"She will be suspended for a week whilst we review whether we can consider taking her back into school. This maybe an expulsion matter, Mrs. Marchand," the headmistress told Gloria.

"You do understand her difficult background, don't you?" Gloria pleaded. "Please take that into consideration during your investigation. She's not a bad girl. I'm sure Cara must have teased her. I'm not excusing her violent outburst, but the other children haven't been kind to her. It's entirely my fault; I invited Cara over to meet Rochelle during the summer holiday, and it didn't go well. You can be sure my husband and I will deal with this at home, but I urge you to consider her future. She's a bright, intelligent girl. Please give her another chance."

Rochelle sat sullenly, in total silence, looking at the floor. She was thinking about what had occurred in the playground. Everything had happened before she knew it. If only Cara hadn't mentioned the car crash and called her an orphan, reminding her that her real parents were dead. Didn't she realise how lucky she was to still have her own parents at home with her every single day?

On the walk home, Gloria didn't utter a word. It was clear to Rochelle that she was extremely angry with her, even though she'd argued her case with the headmistress.

Once home, Derek was called, and Gloria told Rochelle that it was the first time she'd ever disturbed him whilst he was at work.

Derek remained calm as he took the chair opposite Rochelle in the living room.

"Young lady, please explain to me what happened in minute detail."

"I'm sorry, Derek. I didn't mean to make so much blood. I didn't even mean to hit her."

Rochelle shuffled uncomfortably in the armchair: the one Gloria normally sat in.

"What made you do it? I can't imagine why you would want to hurt somebody so badly?"

"She called me an orphan in front of all the other children."

Rochelle tried to shout, but it came out as more of a whisper.

"Go back to the beginning, Rochelle. What has your previous relationship with Cara been like?"

"She hates me, and she's made all the other children hate me. The teacher made her be my buddy, to help me settle in, but she's done exactly the opposite. I try to keep away from all of them. In the playground, I sit on my own reading, but they still won't leave me alone. They tease me and tell me I'm different."

"Okay, Rochelle. Well, at least you do know that what you've done is wrong. Violence is never the answer to any problem. It only makes matters worse.

"This is what's going to happen now. You will write a letter of apology to Cara, and you will also write one to her parents and to the headmistress. Gloria will take the week off work to supervise you here. I will set you work, which I will expect to be completed by the time I get home each day. Any spare time you have will be spent reading. There will be no television for you this week. This weekend, there will be no treats. We will all stay at home and have a quiet time together. In the meantime, I will arrange a meeting with the headmistress and see if I can persuade her, under the circumstances, to take you back after the week's suspension. For the rest of today, you can read in your bedroom and join us downstairs for dinner later."

Before Rochelle crept from the room, she looked back over her shoulder towards them both.

"I'm sorry Derek, and I'm sorry Gloria. I didn't mean to do it," she whispered remorsefully.

Derek made an emotional appeal on Rochelle's behalf to the experienced, grey-haired headmistress, and she agreed to take her back into school after the week's suspension.

Cara's parents had been reasonable about the affair, too, accepting that Cara had not been a total innocent in the unfortunate event. They had reprimanded her for having been unkind to Rochelle.

The week passed by with Rochelle doing everything asked of her. She enjoyed the peace and quiet of being at home with Gloria during the daytime, and worked through the worksheets Derek set for her. She revelled in the attention he showered on her on his return from work, and the praise he gave her for working so hard.

On her return to school, she couldn't help noticing that Cara looked different. The punch had changed the shape of her nose. It was quite swollen, and appeared to have a dent in it.

Rochelle was allocated a new buddy called Susan. The other children were much kinder to her and even allowed her to join in their playground games, but Rochelle was suspicious as to why this was happening.

"Why is everyone being so nice to me, Susan? Even Cara?" Rochelle asked, carefully studying Susan's face.

"Because we didn't understand you before. Cara told us you were nasty and spiteful, and not to play with you. We didn't know how difficult it must be to lose your parents and to have to move to a whole new town and to start a new school ... and, worst of all, to have to have new parents. The headmistress came and explained it all to us."

Rochelle tried her best to fit in after that.

Susan was even invited to come home after school one day to have tea and play in the garden.

However, school still wasn't easy for her. Although her grades were good, she was always getting into trouble for breaking the rules. One day, she decided to skip school altogether, doubling back out of the school gates once Gloria was out of sight. She spent a glorious day by the lake, reading.

Of course, she was found out, and this led to a lot of trouble at school and at home. She had never seen Derek so furious. It scared her; maybe skipping school was not such a good idea if this was the consequence. She now fully understood the meaning of the word Gloria had warned her about when she'd first gone to live with them.

She still got into fights, but it was always with one of the boys, and they could give as good as they got, so it was more balanced and it never led to much trouble. They just called them 'scuffles'.

Compared to the other eight-year-olds in her class, she was still naïve about relationships, though, having missed out on so much real love during her formative years when she'd lived at the children's home.

CHAPTER 9

"Gloria and I like to go to the theatre before Christmas. It's something we do every year, but this year we thought we could take you to see *Disney On Ice* instead. They are putting on a production of *The Lion King*. Would you like to go? Shall I order us some tickets?"

"It sounds exciting, but what is *Disney On Ice*?"

"It's a show that takes place on ice. The skaters will be playing the characters from *The Lion King*," Derek said with a smile on his face.

"Ooh! Yes, please, Derek! I've never seen a show in real life – only on television – and I've never seen anyone skate. I love the story of *The Lion King*."

The week before Christmas, the day came

for them to see the show. Rochelle, whose wardrobe was now full from all the beautiful clothes Gloria had chosen for her, pulled out item after item and threw them on her bed. She had no idea what to wear. What did people wear to see a show?

Gloria entered her bedroom.

"Oh, my goodness! What a mess! What on earth are you doing?"

"What shall I wear, Gloria?"

Rochelle held up a dress against herself.

"You are so funny at times. Let's put some of these clothes back in the wardrobe. Here! You can wear this long-sleeved, rainbow top with the flowers on the front and pair it with some navy leggings."

Once settled in the car, Rochelle asked, "How long will it take us to get there?"

"About an hour, Rochelle. Are you excited?" Derek asked.

"Yes, I can't wait."

She leant forward between the two front seats of the car.

Gloria turned to smile at her.

"Derek's managed to get us front row seats,

so we'll have a great view. It's going to be magical. It's a first for us as well. We've never seen *Disney On Ice* before."

Derek parked the car in a big, underground car park, and they took the lift to the arena.

There were lots of families arriving, and Rochelle beamed. She was part of a family, too. This was her family. She placed her hand in Gloria's.

"From tonight, I'd like to call you Mum. Not Mummy. That's my real Mummy's name."

"That's so sweet, Rochelle. I'd love you to call me Mum."

She winked at Derek.

The arena was already filling with people as they entered. Their seats were right at the front.

Rochelle looked around her.

"I'm so lucky. I'm glad you made me wear my winter coat; it's a little chilly down here by the ice."

The atmosphere around her was full of excitement. It made her feel quite giddy. Children were chatting away with their families.

"Why are there tall, dry grasses placed around the ice, Dad?"

There she'd done it, she'd called Derek, 'Dad'.

"Well, my beautiful daughter, they are part of the set. *The Lion King* is set in Africa."

Daughter!

He'd called her 'daughter'!

The night was getting better and better.

The bright lights dimmed and the ice came to life. The music immersed them, the rhythm touching deep into her soul. Rochelle's eyes widened at the spectacle before her. On the ice, it was night-time, and Rochelle was transported to the pride lands of Africa as a lone voice heralded a new day. The lighting changed to depict daylight and the one voice turned into many. At the back of the rink, there now appeared a distant mountain and skaters appeared from everywhere, covering the ice, characterising a confusion of wildebeest.

On the top of the glittering mountain, a skater appeared dressed as Mufasa, the Lion King. Below was a skater, depicting the furry and inquisitive lion cub, Simba. Rafiki, the shaman of the pride lands, sprinkled dust over Simba, and then picked him up and skated around the whole rink with him raised above his massive shoulders.

Scar appeared from the shadows. The lighting muted and the volume of the orchestra softened as he performed jumps and spins all over the surface of the ice.

Rochelle's face lit up with joy and delight. She was in awe. How amazing to be able to skate on ice. She would love to try. She imagined herself gliding across the icy expanse, people applauding her.

Now, Simba was skating with his father, Mufasa. Every spin or jump Mufasa performed, Simba would copy. Mufasa disappeared and Simba was dancing with his uncle, Scar.

The rink came alive with elephants, hippos, monkeys and giraffes. The music became louder.

A directionless white mist drifted across the ice, and it seemed as though they had all vanished. Suddenly, Rochelle heard chilling laughter and a trio of fierce-looking, filthy hyenas came into view as the mist cleared. The three performed cunning tricks, skating under each other's powerful hind legs. Mufasa spun them around until they were gone from the ice. Simba skated behind Mufasa and followed him off the rink.

The colours changed again, and the ice looked violet. Mufasa reappeared with Simba and they glided around the ice together. Scar watched them from the top of the mountain. The music became louder again. The hyenas were back, performing more tricks. Rochelle was aware that Mufasa had left and Simba was on his own. Scar jumped down from the mountain in a spectacular leap. Rochelle gasped. Claps of thunder made her almost jump out of her skin.

A single spotlight shone at the end of the rink and there was Mufasa, lying still on the ice. A tear tickled Rochelle's rosy cheek as she realised he had died. Simba leant over him and flew into a skating frenzy, jumping and spinning faster than anything she had ever seen.

The song 'Hakuna Matata' blasted around the arena, and the crowd joined in enthusiastically, including Rochelle, who sang at the top of her voice.

Simba sped across the frosty ice to the harsh, craggy mountain. Menacing thunder roared and rolled overhead. Rochelle's beautiful blue eyes lifted skyward as flashes of lightning darted from above across the ice. Scar was at the top of the mountain. Simba climbed towards him, but slipped, hanging in the air at Scar's scant mercy. Somehow Simba managed to pull himself steadily to the top, and a fierce battle ensued between them. Simba lunged at Scar and knocked him off the mountain. He lay still on the ice. Simba let out an ear-splitting roar. He was now the Lion King.

All of the skaters united on the ice and performed the finale together, whilst the crowd went crazy, shouting and applauding. Rochelle, with tears streaming down her cheeks looked at Derek and Gloria.

"Mum! Dad! Thank you! I've never seen anything so special. I love you both."

On the journey home, Rochelle couldn't stop talking.

Animated, she asked, "Can I please have ice-skating lessons? I would love to learn to skate."

Derek replied, "We'll look into it, although we can't promise anything. The nearest ice rink to Windermere is Blackpool, which is an hour's drive away, but if we can find a way around it, the answer will be yes."

He glanced across at Gloria and smiled.

Tucked into her comfy bed that night, Rochelle fell asleep with a sweet smile on her face. She was going to be the best skater there had ever been.

CHAPTER 10

"I'm thrilled to tell you that I've managed to sort out some ice-skating lessons for you, Rochelle. Blackpool is the nearest rink, so it'll take a lot of commitment from Gloria and myself to drive you back and forth. I've booked you a block of six one-hour lessons at 10am on Saturday mornings to see if you like it."

"Oh, Derek! Thank you so much. I'm sure I *will* like it. In fact, I'll love it. You'll see."

"I really hope so. It would be good for you to have a hobby. You spend far too much time reading.

"Can you believe it? A head teacher saying such a thing!" Derek laughed.

On Christmas Eve, Rochelle watched from

the conservatory as a flurry of magical, feather-like snowflakes floated down gracefully from the sky. Tomorrow was going to be Christmas Day. She was so excited. It was going to be the first Christmas she could remember away from the home … the best gift ever!

Gloria was busy cooking in the kitchen. Rochelle had offered to help, but she'd been ushered out.

"I've way too much to prepare. You'll put me off with your constant chatter," she teased.

Rochelle tapped one of the shiny baubles on the Christmas tree that stood next to the fireplace, where a blazing fire was fizzing and spitting. She'd had fun helping Gloria decorate the tree after she and Derek had chosen it together from the Christmas tree farm. She pressed her nose against the leaded window. The snow was blowing in a horizontal blur and then sticking to the grass, turning it a shimmering white. It was all so magical.

"Dad, can we go out and build a snowman?" she asked.

Derek paused from marking some papers.

"It's snowing too heavily at the moment, Rochelle. But, if it's still there in the morning, maybe we could have some fun out there after Christmas dinner."

That night, Rochelle tossed and turned in her cosy bed. She was way too excited to sleep. What presents would she get? What would a family Christmas Day be like? She couldn't wait to find out. As it was a special day, Derek had even told her that she'd be allowed downstairs in her new Christmas pyjamas.

She was awake at six. Did she dare to rise this early? Why not? They wouldn't mind, would they? It *was* Christmas after all!

She took the stairs two at a time and was surprised to find Gloria already pottering around in the kitchen.

"Happy Christmas, Rochelle! Look outside! The snow's still there. It's a white Christmas! How special is that on your first Christmas with us …?

"Derek's awake, by the way. Go and knock on our bedroom door. He said he'd get up as soon as you did."

Rochelle darted back upstairs to Gloria and Derek's bedroom and banged on the door.

"Dad, come on! It's Christmas," she shouted.

She ran downstairs, followed closely by Derek.

"Take your time! You'll break your neck."

Rochelle was far too excited to heed his warning and ran straight into the living room.

There were lots of beautifully-wrapped presents under the Christmas tree, which was filling the room with its natural sweet pine fragrance.

"Are these all for me, Dad?"

"Well, not all of them, silly. I know there are some for Gloria; remember we went shopping and bought her a present from you? I'm hoping there are some there for me, as well."

Gloria handed them both a cup of tea, and Derek poured a little whisky into his.

"A special treat on Christmas morning,' he said.

Rochelle selected a large present from under the tree and read out the message on the label.

"*To Rochelle, with love on your first Christmas with us, from Mum and Dad.*

"Am I allowed to open it now?" she asked.

"Yes! We'll open a few now, and then have some toast before we open the rest. There are so many under the tree," Gloria said.

Rochelle tore at the wrapping paper. She was so excited.

"Wow! It's a globe. I've always wanted my own globe."

"It's a special one, Rochelle. It's a standard globe in the daytime, but, at night, a sensor switches on the LED lights that illuminate the key stars, so you can learn the constellations," Derek said, getting up from his armchair to show her how it worked.

"Can I give Mum her present now – the one we bought together, Dad?"

"Of course, you can. It's the one at the front with the silver wrapping."

Rochelle handed the package to Gloria.

"I chose this myself, with Derek's, I mean Dad's, help."

Gloria opened the wrapping, careful not to tear the paper.

"How kind of you. My first ever present from you."

"It's a pair of cosy slippers you can heat up

in the microwave. They'll keep your feet nice and warm," Rochelle declared.

"Thank you, darling. They're just what I needed. I'll throw my old ones away and pop these lovely new ones straight on my feet."

Rochelle beamed.

"I got you a present too, Dad. I wrapped this one all by myself."

Derek smiled at her.

"Thank you, precious."

He squeezed it.

"I reckon it's a book."

"Open it! Open it!" Rochelle shrieked excitedly.

"I am," he laughed.

"It's a journal. Look it says: *'Dear dad, from me to you.'* You can write about you and me in it."

"What a special gift. I shall treasure it for ever, and I'll write about lots of happy memories in it."

He winked across at Gloria.

"Let's have some toast now, and while I'm at it, I'll pop the turkey into the oven. We can open the rest of our presents afterwards."

After gobbling down the toast as quickly as she could, Rochelle tore open her next present. It was a big sticky note pad.

"You can do some drawings and stick them on your bedroom wall. It will make the room more your own," Derek said.

Rochelle hugged them both.

"Thank you so much! This is the best Christmas ever."

The next present she opened was a book: '*The Foolish King*' by Mark Price and Martin Brown.

"It will help you learn how to play chess. It's a game I love, but Gloria's not so keen. So, when you've learnt, we can play together."

Rochelle was already tearing the paper off her next present. It was a chess and draughts set.

"Wow! Now you can teach me the game chess," she declared.

Next, Derek passed Rochelle a large present. It was obviously a box, but what could be inside it?

"This is our main present to you. We hope

you like it."

She tore at the paper.

"What is it? What's inside?"

Her mouth fell wide open.

"Oh my God! My own ice skates! I can't believe it. My own skates!"

She ran and hugged them both.

"You've made me so happy."

After showering, she put on the new red dress Gloria had bought for her to wear on Christmas Day, and they all sat around the dining room table to eat their meal. Rochelle had never tasted such a delicious Christmas dinner. There was turkey, crisp roast potatoes, mashed potatoes, pigs in blankets, stuffing, carrots, peas, Brussels sprouts and cauliflower cheese, all topped off with a thick, luscious gravy. She cleared her plate, but when Gloria offered her Christmas pudding, she laughed.

"Mum, there's no room in my tummy for anything else. I'm about to burst."

Afterwards, she helped Gloria clear the table and do the washing-up. Gloria washed, and she dried. This routine had been established for a while now, and she never complained. This was what was expected of her. It was worth it … to live here, and be part of a family.

When they'd finished, Derek had fallen asleep on the sofa in the living room, and Gloria said she could do with a nap too, so Rochelle took herself off into the conservatory to read her new book. She glanced out of the window. It had stopped snowing, but outside everything was white. Maybe after their nap, they would build a snowman with her?

He was the first to wake. After flexing his limbs, he crept into the conservatory, trying not to wake Gloria.

"Shall we go and play in the snow? Let's leave Gloria to sleep a little longer. She's worked hard preparing all of our Christmas dinner.

"Go and change into something more suitable, but make sure you put some warm clothes on. You'll need your thick, winter coat and your furry hat, scarf and mittens. Oh, and don't forget your red wellies."

Rochelle shot upstairs, but was back in no

time. She headed outside into the pure white, thick snowy carpet, and enjoyed making the first footsteps in the undisturbed snow. Derek followed behind her. He picked up some snow, formed it into a snowball and threw it at her. She squealed with delight, and fired one straight back at him.

She looked down at her red mittens.

"Look at the beautiful crystals on my mittens, Dad," she exclaimed.

Derek winked at her, and then lay down in the middle of the garden, moving his arms up and down in the soft snow. Rochelle lay down next to him and did the same.

When they got up, she noticed that there were two winged angels depicted next to each other in the snow.

Afterwards, they rolled two large snowballs, the larger one for the snowman's body, and the smaller one for his head. Derek found two small, roundish stones for his eyes, and they made his nose and a mouth out of some sticks. Rochelle removed the scarf from her own neck and placed it around the snowman's. Then they both stood back and admired their work.

"He's magnificent. What shall we name him,

Rochelle?"

"Sticks," she replied. "We'll call him Sticks."

"Let's go back inside, shall we? I'll make us both a hot chocolate. I'm freezing now," Derek declared.

Gloria greeted them at the door.

"What a fabulous snowman you've made!"

"He's called Sticks, Mum," Rochelle said, as she pulled off all of her wet clothing.

"Shall we sit and watch a film now? I've found one I think we'll all enjoy. It's by Dr. Seuss and it's called *How the Grinch Stole Christmas*."

"It sounds like fun," Rochelle said, heading into the lounge.

She cuddled up with Gloria on the sofa while they all watched the film together, and when it had finished, Rochelle made them laugh by singing, "*You're a mean one, Mr Grinch.*"

Afterwards, Gloria made them some turkey and beetroot sandwiches, and before she knew it, it was time for bed. She kissed them both good night and went upstairs feeling happy and content. She was asleep almost before her head hit the pillow; it had been the perfect Christmas Day with her new Mum and Dad.

The following week, it was time for her first skating lesson at the ice rink in Blackpool. She couldn't contain herself; she was so excited. Derek had found her some ice-skating to watch on TV, and she had studied the moves in great detail, noting how they held their hands and glided across the ice like graceful swans. She decided there and then that she wanted to be an Olympic ice-skater like Alina Zagitova.

The drive to Blackpool seemed to take forever.

"Can't we go any faster, Dad?" she asked.

Derek laughed.

"No! And it wouldn't matter if we did. Your lesson is at ten, and we'll be there well before that."

In actual fact, they arrived twenty minutes early. She had practised putting on her skates in her bedroom lots of times, and with the guards on the blades had already learnt how to stand and take short walks in them.

She immediately put on her skates and

strode off towards the barrier at the near side of the rink to watch the 9 o'clock lessons, which were still taking place.

Derek and Gloria went off to the rink café to get a cup of tea.

A girl approached Rochelle at the side of the barrier.

"Hi, I'm Vanessa Eads. Are you new? I've not seen you here before."

"Hi! Yeah! It's my first time. I'm so excited. I'm Rochelle … Rochelle Erickson."

"You'll love it. It's so much fun. I've been coming for about six weeks now. I'm going to be an Olympic champion one day," she said, standing on one skate to show off her new skills.

"Oh! How fab! Me too … even though I haven't been on the ice yet. I'm determined, you see. It's been my dream since I watched *The Lion King* on ice."

"Oh! I went to see *The Lion King* as well. It was fab, wasn't it?

"What's your coach's name?" she asked running her gloved hand along the barrier.

"Juliet Brandon. I think that's what Dad said her name was."

"Well, you're lucky to have got in with her. She's an excellent coach."

She switched legs and stood on the opposite skate.

Rochelle smiled at Vanessa. She seemed nice. She liked her already.

"Maybe we'll become skating friends?" she said.

"Sure! I like you. You're pretty.

"Here's your coach coming over now. That's Juliet … the one with the dark, cherry red hair. She dyes it, you can't really have hair that colour."

Juliet skated over to the two girls.

"Hi, Vanessa. Is this Rochelle you're talking to?"

"Yeah! This is Rochelle. It's her first time ever on the ice."

"Hi, Rochelle. I'm Juliet Brandon. It's nice to meet you. Where are your Mum and Dad?"

Rochelle pointed upwards to the window of the first-floor café.

"They're in there, watching from behind the glass. Mum was freezing and wanted a cup of tea to warm her up."

"Come on, then! Let's get you on the ice. Take off your guards and leave them at the side here," Juliet instructed.

Rochelle held Juliet's outstretched hand and allowed her to lead her onto the ice. This was the moment she'd practised over and over in her head. She was invigorated. This was so exciting.

"Now, I know it sounds silly, but the first thing I'm going to teach you is how to fall over," Juliet announced. "Falling is part of the sport, so it's important you know how to fall. This will mean you'll have less chance of getting injured. If you're losing your balance, bend your knees and squat into a dipped position. Lean forwards, fall sideways onto the ice, and place your hand on your lap. As soon as you fall, roll over onto your hands and knees. Then, one at a time, place your feet between your hands and push yourself back up to the standing position."

After practising this a few times, Juliet led Rochelle by her mittened hand around the slippery rink until she was obviously feeling comfortable on the ice … and, before she knew it, Rochelle was gliding around on her own.

"This is amazing," she shouted.

"There you go. You're a natural. We'll soon make a skater out of you."

Juliet clapped her hands together.

Next, Juliet taught her how to stop and she practised more gliding. Juliet showed her how to extend the motion into what she called stroking. The last part of her lesson was to learn swizzles.

The hour was over way too fast for Rochelle. She didn't want to leave the ice.

"There's a public session now, so if your parents agree, you could stay on the ice and practise some more.

"You've done well. Did you enjoy it?"

"I loved it, Juliet. Thank you. I'll see you next week," she said with a huge smile spreading across her face.

She skated off the ice to find Derek and Gloria.

"Did you see me? I can skate. It was brilliant! Can I stay for the public session and practise some more?"

"Aren't you tired? Don't you need a little rest?" Gloria asked, looking at her empty cup on the table in front of her.

"No! Not at all, Mum. Look there's Vanessa, the girl I met. She's staying on to practise a bit more. Please can I?"

Derek and Gloria laughed, and in unison said, "Yes."

Rochelle whizzed off to catch up with Vanessa.

"Hey! Wait for me, Vanessa!" she shouted.

They held hands and skated together around the rink. Vanessa was a lot faster, but Rochelle was determined to keep up with her.

After that, skating became her way of life … her release. The six-week trial period had ended with Juliet explaining to her parents that she had a natural talent, with the potential to go a long way. It wasn't long before she was spending all her Saturdays skating. Gloria and Derek would drop her off at ten for her first lesson, and afterwards she would skate with Vanessa until lunchtime. After lunch in the rink café, the two girls would have another private lesson and then stay for the afternoon public session, as well.

Derek and Gloria would spend the day in Blackpool and collect her at four, never once complaining about her passion for skating and how time-consuming it was to their own lives.

Not long after her ninth birthday, Juliet entered her into her first major competition.

"Are you nervous, Rochelle?" Gloria asked. "Just the thought of you stepping out on the ice to compete makes me feel nervous."

"I'm more excited than nervous. My tummy's doing somersaults."

She hopped from one foot to the other as they stood at the side of the barrier.

At the warm-up, Juliet said to her, "When it's your turn, go out there and have fun. Show off a little and enjoy the experience. But make sure you do your best."

As she waited her turn to skate, Gloria fussed over her hair.

"We are so proud of you. My goodness ... I don't know about your tummy, but mine's got a whole bunch of butterflies flying around in it."

"Remember to skate against yourself, not the other skaters. And don't be disappointed, if you don't win. If you come off the ice knowing that you've done your best, you should feel happy, no matter where you're placed," Derek advised her.

"I know, but wouldn't it be great if one of us won against the girls from the other rinks? We *do* have an advantage with the competition being held here, at the rink where we train."

"How many girls are there in the competition?" Gloria asked.

"Ten! I'm number five to skate, and Vanessa is number seven," she said, holding up her hand to show five fingers.

At that moment, an announcement came over the tannoy.

"We are pleased to be staging the British Junior Championship competition for girls aged ten and under. The first skater to perform today is Zena Fields. Please give her a warm round of support."

Rochelle watched as Zena skated onto the ice. The first thing she compared was their outfits. She liked the pale pink costume the girl was wearing, but it made her look a little bit like a princess. She preferred the Tiffany Blue one that Gloria had made for her to wear today.

She studied the girls' programme in detail.

She was good, but not as good as Vanessa.

Soon, it was time for Rochelle to skate. She entered the ice through the skater's entry door and skated out into the middle of the rink to strike her initial pose. She indicated her readiness to the judges and relaxed her shoulders.

Her choice of music, '*Diamonds*' by Rihanna, echoed around the ice rink. She floated around gracefully and struck an arabesque around the wide top end of the rink, her slim leg held high posed in the perfect position. After a few soft turns, she skated backwards, building up maximum speed, and then she executed her first jump: a double lutz. She nailed the landing! From the forward, outside, sharp blade, extreme edge of one skate, she launched an axel, turning one and a half times in the air and landing on the backward, outside edge of the other skate, just as Juliet had taught her. This was immediately followed by a salchow.

She turned into a cross foot spin, holding herself upright, crossing her free leg behind the skating foot, and spinning as fast as she could. She chased across the ice, with gliding steps, one foot displacing the other.

The music had become part of her and she

drifted off into it, just like a diamond, shining bright in her blue dress. She demonstrated her elegant footwork, leading into a toe loop, with a full turn in the air, initiated with the help of her supporting foot.

She then turned into a pancake spin, her free leg canting towards her athletic body and her upper body bent over it, forming a dramatic illusion of her body as a pancake.

Gaining tremendous speed again, she performed a double toe loop, followed by a double salchow. She flew forward, high in the air in a lutz, again nailing the landing.

Crossing the rink at speed, she leapt high into a double loop, flying into a butterfly spin, her near-horizontal body position and a scissoring leg action in the air, with a two-foot, twisting take-off.

As the music ended, she timed it to perfection to lay on the ice in the position of an angel, a smile forming across her face.

She got up to take a bow towards the judges and skated off the ice, beaming. It was a brilliant performance; the crowd went wild applauding her.

Juliet was waiting attentively by the skater's door. She was dressed confidently in gold and scarlet, and was trying her best not to show how nervous she was. She patted Rochelle on her perfectly upright back.

"You pulled it off! Well done! You were amazing."

Rochelle thanked her and went off in search of Gloria and Derek, wishing Vanessa good luck as she passed the girl waiting for her turn to skate.

Standing with Derek and Gloria she watched the other skaters perform.

"We are so proud of you. Your skating was incredible. It's been worth all the commitment and hard work. You stand a good chance of winning a medal," Gloria said.

Out of the skaters to follow, Vanessa shone, giving a fantastic, well-polished performance. Rochelle was pleased for her friend; it would have been horrible to see her fall.

A centre-stage podium was manoeuvred out onto the ice, and the senior judge made the official announcement.

"In third place is Hayleigh Darby. In second place is Rochelle Erickson. And in first place is Vanessa Eads."

Rochelle jumped in the air as Derek and

Gloria tried to hug her.

"Second! I got second place! Can you believe it? And Vanessa got first!"

She held onto the barrier to steady herself.

Vanessa came alongside her at the skater's entry door, and they gave each other a congratulatory hug.

"We did it, Rochelle! We got first and second place. I'm British Junior Champion and you're the runner-up," Vanessa said.

They crossed the ice together and took their positions on the makeshift podium. The judge congratulated them all, then placed a bronze medal on a ribbon around Hayleigh's neck, a silver one around Rochelle's and handed Vanessa a large, silver trophy.

Back at school, although the children were more pleasant to her, she still didn't have many friends, preferring to hang around with Susan. But even Susan didn't really understand Rochelle's obsession with skating. Only Vanessa understood, but she didn't go to the same school.

By the age of ten, Rochelle's passion for skating had taken over the whole family's lives. To her, there was no better way to spend her whole weekend skating on the glittering, cold ice, spinning so fast that she felt like she was drifting and floating above it. When she leaped in the air, she actually felt as though she was flying.

Juliet had recommended that she take gymnastics and dance lessons to improve her body awareness and grace, so after school on Tuesdays, she attended gymnastics, and, on Thursdays, she had dance lessons. Her strength and confidence were growing daily, and she loved these additional classes, but nowhere near as much as she did her skating tuition.

Vanessa had begun to train on both days, too, so the girls spent all of their weekends together, receiving their one-to-one lessons from their individual coaches, but also attending the public sessions and taking lunch with one another each day.

"Will we ever make it to the Winter Olympics, Rochelle?" Vanessa sighed as they stood in the lunch queue at the rink café one very rainy Sunday.

"Of course, we will! There's not even the slightest doubt in my mind," Rochelle answered.

The summer holidays arrived and Derek kept to his word, taking the family camping for a week. They stayed on a quiet campsite, away from the crowds at a small village called Lazonby, on the River Eden. The weather was perfect and the rich woodland scenery around them was stunning. Rochelle was so excited to be on her first ever camping trip.

On the first morning, Derek cooked them a delicious breakfast of bacon rolls on the camping stove, and afterwards he told Rochelle to put on her hiking boots as they were heading off on a long hike.

They crossed Eden Bridge which led to the tiny, picturesque market town of Kirkoswald. Derek pointed out the grander Georgian buildings as they passed close to St. Oswald's church. As they ambled along, Gloria taught Rochelle the names of the local flora that grew abundantly along the well-trodden paths.

Moving on to Little Salkeld, they stopped at the watermill: a working mill, which still provided the flour for the bread and cakes sold at the tearoom where they had afternoon tea. By now ravenous, Rochelle filled her tummy with delicious homemade scones, strawberry jam and clotted cream, declaring,

"This is so yummy."

Afterwards, they took a quick look around some caves, before Derek suggested they head back to the campsite before it became dark.

Back at the site, Derek lit a campfire and cooked a barbecue. Rochelle loved sitting outside in the dark, with Derek pointing out the different stars sprinkled in the night sky. Later, tucked up in her warm, comfortable sleeping bag, inside her own zipped compartment, Rochelle fell asleep listening to the cries of the local fauna … the serenade of the night.

After breakfast the following morning, they went to a bicycle hire shop and rented mountain bikes. Rochelle had learned to ride a bike at the home, and had passed her cycling proficiency test at school the year before. She was super excited at the prospect of them all riding bikes together.

By lunchtime they were hungry and thirsty, so they parked their bikes outside a pub named The Shepherds Inn and ordered lunch. Derek had a superb-looking, American-style burger, Rochelle a cottage pie, and Gloria fish and chips. Their appetites were huge and the food was good, so all their plates were cleared in no time. After a short rest, they continued their pleasant bike ride.

From the pub, they rode along the Pennine Cycleway, through Melmerby to Gamblesby, towards the river, and they crossed the charming bridge over the River Eden back to the campsite.

By now, Rochelle was struggling to keep up. She was exhausted and her legs and bottom ached. So, as soon as they'd eaten dinner, she asked if she could have an early night.

The third day of their special holiday, Gloria suggested they go for a scenic drive to rest their aching limbs after their intense physical efforts of the previous two days.

They drove to Penrith. Derek found a parking space, and they ventured into the town to amble slowly around the shops. After a while, they sat down outside a café, resting and drinking tea. But, the adjacent park gardens lured Rochelle in, and she was allowed to go off on her own to explore them.

Soon after, they drove back to the campsite and Gloria prepared a late lunch. The endless sunny afternoon was spent lazing around, reading and sunbathing in the glorious, late-afternoon sunshine.

In the calm stillness of the evening, they

walked to the local pub and sat in the shadowy beer garden for dinner. That night, relaxed and happy, Rochelle fell asleep in no time.

The following day, Derek told Rochelle that they had a special treat booked for her. They were to drive to Troutbeck for Rochelle to go pony trekking.

Rochelle was ecstatic; she had never ridden a pony.

A young lady helped her onto a handsome, little pony and walked alongside, holding the reins. Rochelle was thrilled as they headed along a quiet bridle path past a twentieth-century pub. The picturesque views opened to a stunning sight of the magnificent fells. She felt as though she were on top of the world. They continued on, passing through vast farmland with dirty-yellow sheep and she enjoyed looking out for the plentiful wildlife all around her. The lady who was leading the pony let go of the reins, and Rochelle learned how to make him walk and trot.

Back at the tent, she lay reading in the late afternoon sun. Her skin had turned a beautiful, golden brown and it dawned on her how lucky she was to have been adopted by such wonderful parents.

With only two days of the holiday left, she woke and stretched. What would they do today? She loved the fact that every day had been an amazing surprise, only finding out each morning what Gloria and Derek had planned for the day ahead. She burst out of the tent, which was now looking a bit dishevelled, to find Derek cooking their regular bacon rolls. He informed her that they were going for a train ride on La'al Ratty, a local, well-loved, little railway line. She already knew about La'al Ratty. They had taught her about it at school, and there were photographs of it in one of the long school corridors.

They sat in an open carriage, with no roof or windows, the wind blowing through her hair. She was exhilarated as they took the journey from Eskdale to Ravenglass. Derek seemed pleased that she was showing such a keen interest.

The final day of their holiday turned out to be the best. Derek and Gloria had told her that today was to be a special surprise. As they drove along in the car, all she knew was that their destination was Keswick.

The whole day turned out to be amazing! They parked by the lake and met a guide who told them he was going to teach them about the 'great outdoors'. He explained they would be joining another family for the day's adventure. Rochelle couldn't believe her eyes when she saw Vanessa and her parents walking towards them.

So, this was the surprise! Derek and Gloria had arranged all this! The two girls hugged. It was a surprise for Vanessa as well.

The girls had so much fun being taught some basic survival skills. They learned how to make substantial shelters from trees, how to light fires using only flint and steel, and how to collect and boil water to cook food. They were taught how to tie intricate knots and some useful knife skills. The experienced guide pointed out certain plants and trees, many of which Rochelle already knew the names of, as Gloria had already taught her.

Shattered at the end of their perfect day, the girls hugged one another a sad goodbye as they climbed back into their parents' cars.

The tent was already packed away, so they headed home to Windermere, having had a fantastic holiday.

It was at that moment that Rochelle realised that she was loved.

By her eleventh birthday, Rochelle's motivation to skate and become an Olympic champion had strengthened even further. Her friendship with Vanessa had blossomed and they cherished each other as close friends, spending whatever time they could practising their skating at the rink.

By then, Rochelle had taken the title of British Junior Champion, with the positions on the podium being reversed compared to the previous year. They were both too old at eleven to compete again for the junior title, and they were now working towards competing at senior level, spending more and more time at the rink.

One Sunday, as they sat eating their lunch in the café, Vanessa turned to Rochelle.

"It's getting harder, now … the skating. Will we ever be good enough to enter the senior competition?"

"Of course, we will, Vanessa! We'll ace it! You'll see," she said picking up a slice of pizza.

Later that year, the two girls were dizzy with

excitement when they discovered that they were to attend the same senior school in Keswick. Derek had said it wasn't a good idea for Rochelle to attend the school where he was head teacher, as it might make her more vulnerable. So, she was going to the one that was a little further away.

For Vanessa, who lived in Cockermouth, it was her first-choice school.

On arrival at Meadows Ridge, however, Rochelle was mortified to discover that Vanessa wasn't in her class. She had imagined them being able to sit next to each other and had been so excited at the prospect. In reality, the classroom seemed massive, and the ceilings were much higher than she'd expected. It was all very confusing.

She had arrived late, even though Gloria had put her on the right bus in Windermere, but the traffic had been awful. The other children had already taken their seats at their desks. Her eyes searched around the room for Vanessa, and having realised that she wasn't there, she took the only available chair.

The male teacher was explaining a weekly timetable and how they were to move from one class to another for their lessons. Maybe Vanessa would be in one of those other lessons? She hoped so, as she glanced around once more to check she hadn't missed her.

After copying the timetable from the blackboard, they all headed off for the first lesson of the day: English. The teacher had explained they'd been put into three sets, based on how well they'd done in their junior school exams. Rochelle was in Set 1 for all of her subjects.

As they all headed into the enormous corridor to find their relevant classroom, Rochelle was further horrified to discover that she was the only girl to be wearing a pleated, grey skirt. All the other girls were wearing trousers.

She was desperate to use the toilet, but she didn't know where they were, and anyway, she didn't want to be late for English. She was sure Vanessa would also be in Set 1, and she didn't want somebody else to already be sitting next to her.

The classroom wasn't too difficult to find. Being one of the first to arrive, she took a seat near the back, and placed her bag on the one next to her, hoping to reserve it for Vanessa. As the other children poured into the room, she scanned their faces looking for her friend.

Another girl approached and asked if she could sit next to her.

"No! I'm sorry! This seat's reserved for my friend."

The classroom filled with students who all seemed to have an abundance of energy. There was no sign of Vanessa, and now she found that she was the only one not paired in one of the double desks. It finally dawned on her that Vanessa wasn't in Set 1.

As the gloomy morning passed, she consoled herself with the idea that she would at least see Vanessa at lunchtime. However, that wasn't what Rochelle expected either. Checking her timetable, she discovered that she only had a thirty-minute lunch break. It took her five minutes to pack her grey school bag, and a further five minutes to find the toilets, where she heaved, due to the smell of stale urine. Following this, she headed to the canteen, where she worked out that she only had 15 minutes to get her food and eat it, as she would need to allow five minutes to get to the first afternoon lesson: French.

The queue in the bright, noisy canteen was massive, and she still couldn't see Vanessa. As she stood in the queue, she kept checking her watch as the precious lunch break slipped away. By the time she was at the front of the queue, chosen her lunch and found a seat, she had to gobble her food, else she would have been late for French. Where on earth was Vanessa?

As the end of the day came around, and she waited at the bus stop for the bus back to Windermere not having seen Vanessa once, she decided it had been one of her most miserable days ever. She also had piles of homework to do when she got home.

Senior school stinks, she declared to herself.

Worse still, she wasn't going to be able to attend her after-school gymnastics and dance lessons, as they were for junior school pupils only.

On her return home, she raced to the phone to call Vanessa. Gloria and Derek still hadn't allowed her to have a mobile, declaring her still too young to be responsible for one. She had been promised one for her twelfth birthday.

Sitting on the bottom stair in the hallway, she dialled Vanessa's number.

"Where were you today? Were you ill? Why did you miss our first day?"

"I didn't! I was in school. I looked for you all day, but I couldn't see you. The corridors seemed about ten miles long."

The conversation concluded with them having discovered that Vanessa was in Set 2, so none of their lessons would be together, and their lunch periods were at different times. too.

Rochelle arched her fingers over her mouth and blew out a long breath.

"Well, you'll have to work mighty hard to get into Set 1, or else I'll have to do some rubbish work to get into your set.

"I'll see you on Saturday at the rink. Love you!" she concluded.

"Love you, too," Vanessa replied.

The phone went dead. Rochelle stood up and replaced the handset on its base.

During the period up to her twelfth birthday, Rochelle went through a lot of changes as she became more and more aware of her body. In particular, she insisted that Gloria buy her some almond oil to put on her nails, so that they'd grow longer, like some of the more popular girls in school.

CHAPTER 11

By the age of 13, Rochelle was hanging out with what she considered to be the cool kids from school. She often deliberately missed the school bus home so that she could go to the local park and swig bottles of WKD, get tipsy and fool around with her friends. She had a mobile phone now, so it was easy to send Gloria a text saying that she'd be home later than expected due to an unplanned school activity.

Gloria had noticed that Rochelle was a little grumpier than she used to be, but her worries had been eased when Derek reassured her that it was a normal stage for most 13-year-olds to go through. He told her he witnessed it every day in his own school. Gloria nagged Rochelle about always being on her phone, but again Derek said it was pretty normal.

She was beginning to get attention from boys and was enjoying teasing them and chatting to them after school. However, she regretted sending a picture of herself in her bra and knickers to Dylan Tod, who had shown it around school.

Vanessa was annoying her of late, making her angry by always talking about skating; it was getting on her nerves. Rochelle's body had become her shrine, and she spent ages getting ready for school each day, trying to make herself look as good as she could. She no longer wanted to go skating all the time, and had cut out her Sunday lessons altogether.

Shutting herself off in her bedroom one Sunday, Rochelle couldn't stop crying. She was so miserable. The week before, she'd had a massive argument with Vanessa, and they were no longer speaking to one another. She'd begun to feel that her life was too narrow ... that she was trapped.

She'd lost her purse at the skating rink the previous day with a £10 note inside it, and she didn't have the heart to tell Gloria and Derek. She knew that they were good people, and that they did their best for her, but it wasn't enough. Everything was pretence ... a lie ...

an act. The world was unreal … like living in a dream.

Gloria knocked her bedroom door and entered.

"How's the book project going for school?" she asked.

"Why do you want to know? My academic grades are always really good, so why would you care?"

Gloria was taken aback! Rochelle had never spoken to her like that before.

"I was only checking that you're okay. Have you been crying? What's the matter?"

She moved further into the bedroom.

"Nothing! Get out of my room and leave me alone!" Rochelle exploded.

"I don't know what's got into you, but that's no way to speak to me," Gloria huffed and walked out, closing Rochelle's door behind her.

On the following Monday morning, Rochelle didn't get ready at her normal time. She hadn't the slightest intention of going to her lousy school today. She would tell Gloria that she had a migraine and needed to rest.

She lay back on her bed and studied her walls. Gone were her childish drawings, now replaced with posters: a black and white one of Marilyn Monroe, and another one of Che Guevara. She'd picked it because it had *REVOLUTION!* boldly printed across it. She didn't understand what it meant, but it looked mighty cool. Gloria hated it.

On the opposite wall, she had a large print of some intelligent-looking dogs sitting around a table playing cards, which she found amusing.

After she had persuaded Gloria that she wasn't well enough to attend school, she watched them both leave for work from her bedroom window. Now, she could do what she liked with nobody to nag or complain at her.

She grabbed her mobile and set a status on Facebook: *'Life's shit!!!'*

This would show who cared about her.

She checked and rechecked her phone, but not one single person had even liked her post, let alone commented on it. Anxiety was growing inside her. Nobody liked her and nobody cared, not even Vanessa!

She jumped out of her bed and sat down at her dressing table. She stared into the mirror and examined herself. Her. once beautiful, golden blonde hair now looked coarse and thin, and it had lost its natural curl.

It's not surprising that nobody likes me looking like this, she thought.

Full of despair, she now secretly wished she'd gone to school so that she could have hung out in the park afterwards. Shc needed a way to switch off this negativity. It wasn't doing her any good.

She knew that Vanessa was skating at a far higher level than she was, and this was part of the problem. She'd begun to suffer flashbacks of her real parents' fatal road accident. She was angry and upset, but she didn't know what to do with all these new, raw emotions.

Some of the most popular girls at school now had boyfriends, and although she hung out with the boys, not one of them had shown any real interest in her, other than Dylan Tod. But look what he'd gone and done ... sharing the photo of her in her underwear ... making her look like a tart.

She decided to send Vanessa a text.

She typed in, *'Hey, how are you? I'm not great.'*

and hit send.

To avoid waiting forever for a reply that may never come, she threw her mobile phone onto her bed and headed downstairs to the kitchen to make herself a cup of tea.

Afterwards, she chose an action-packed book from her book shelf and tried to read huddled in her favourite chair in the conservatory. But where she had once found solace in this sort of activity, now there was none. She couldn't focus on the words, and the monotonous sound of their elderly neighbour mowing his perfect, green lawn was driving her crazy.

Restless, she headed back to her bedroom and checked her phone. No response from Vanessa. Yes, they'd had an almighty argument, but it had been about nothing. All she'd done was to tell Vanessa to stop being so precious about everything … to lighten up … life wasn't only about skating.

Enraged, she hurled her phone at the bedroom wall. She knew by the sound of the impact that it had smashed. She lay on her bed sobbing, wishing her real parents were alive. This wasn't the life she was supposed to have had.

She heard the key turning in the front door.

"Rochelle, I got out of work early, so I could be at home with you today. Where are you?" Gloria shouted.

Rochelle dried her eyes, grabbed the broken phone and pushed it underneath a pile of knickers in her underwear drawer.

She opened her bedroom door a few inches.

"I'm in my room, but my head still hurts, so I'd rather be left alone."

She could hear Gloria coming upstairs.

"I'm drenched. The wind and rain were atrocious on my way home, and my umbrella was useless against them."

"Oh, it's raining? Hadn't noticed," she said and closed her bedroom door.

Gloria stood resolutely behind it.

"I know you have a migraine, Rochelle, but maybe if your head and the weather both improve we could go into town and do some shopping later. We could get you some new trainers."

Her decision was made. New trainers … or lie in bed all day feigning a migraine?

She shouted through the closed door.

"I'll be ready in an hour. My head's improving."

"Great," Gloria replied. "I've put aside £50. That should be enough to get you a pair you like."

"I'll get ready now, Mum. I'm hungry. I haven't had any breakfast. Can you make me some lunch before we go, please?"

"Sure, I can!" Gloria replied with a wry smile. How amazing that Rochelle's migraine had miraculously disappeared!

Rochelle washed and dressed, and was downstairs in no time. She quickly gobbled down the triangular-shaped ham sandwiches Gloria had made for her and stood by the front door.

"Come on, Mum! I'm ready!"

Rochelle took her large, yellow hat from the cloak stand and placed it on her head.

"Do you have to wear that?"

"I like it. It makes me stand out from the crowd," she said, pulling it down even tighter.

As they headed along the road towards town, Gloria asked, "So what's gone wrong? Why have you been so moody, and what's the real reason you didn't want to go to school today?"

"I'm sorry, Mum. I've been missing my real parents lately. I can't stop myself from wondering how my life might have been ..."

Gloria placed her arm around Rochelle and pulled her closer.

"Try not to dwell on it, darling. It won't do you any favours. You can't bring them back, I'm afraid."

CHAPTER 12

Vanessa's belief in Rochelle had changed. She knew she'd been through a lot, and she'd seen a lot of horrible things, but she'd been acting very weirdly lately.

Since the massive argument they'd had, she was far more cautious around Rochelle than she used to be. They were speaking again now, but she was far more careful about confiding in her.

She envied Rochelle's infinite energy, but sometimes she found it eye-rollingly annoying. She couldn't understand why Rochelle wasn't as motivated in her skating as she'd previously been. She'd noticed that she was no longer skating at the same level, and this made her unhappy. She was annoyed with her. It had been far more fun when they'd competed with each other to be the best. It had made her want to keep improving.

She was still bitter about the argument. Rochelle had said some cruel things about her. She'd since told her that she regretted those things, but she believed that she was only being nice to her for selfish reasons. She wasn't convinced that Rochelle was a genuine friend anymore.

She envied Rochelle at school. She didn't put half the effort into her work as she did, and yet her grades were always good. Rochelle remained in the top set for everything, whilst she couldn't seem to work her way out of the second set in any of her subjects.

But, she still hoped that they would be best friends again, one day.

Always being late for everything, including her skating lessons, had become a problem for Vanessa. It was made worse by the fact that it was never her own fault. She was always waiting on her mother who was never ready on time, always applying a little more make-up or changing her outfit.

Today was no different; she was dropped off at the rink 20 minutes late for her lesson.

After quickly putting on her skates, she hurried over to her coach.

"Sorry for keeping you waiting. My mother wasn't ready again."

"It's not good enough, Vanessa. You're wasting my time, as well as your own.

"If you want to be considered for the American scholarship next summer, you need to be on time for your lessons."

Plaits bobbing, Vanessa took her starting position for the latest programme she and her coach had been practising together. Her double jumps now perfected, she was attempting triples, as well as a split jump. This was resulting in a lot of falls, and after only five minutes of her lesson, she was off the ice, in tears and considerable pain, sporting a bruised right elbow.

Her coach followed her to make sure she hadn't suffered any serious injury, but, as she tested Vanessa's arm, a whiff of her coach's cheap floral perfume made Vanessa nauseous. Conscious of the vomit clawing at her throat, she experienced an attack of acute anxiety. Her heart was racing, her stomach was in knots and sweat beads were appearing on her forehead. Her face turned bright red, her mouth was dry and she was filled with an absolute sense of dread.

Her coach enquired, "Are you okay? You look awful."

Without answering, Vanessa dashed to the cloakroom and locked herself in a cubicle.

A minute later, she heard the cloakroom door opening. It was Rochelle.

"Vanessa! What's the matter?" she cried. "Your coach has just fetched me off the ice. She said you might be having a panic attack.

"Come on out! Let's have a hug. I miss you."

CHAPTER 13

When Vanessa took to the ice, her natural talent became a combination of art and athleticism. Her artistic expression shone, as she glided across the ice. The intricate manoeuvres she performed were outstanding and were becoming more and more elaborate. She held a presence that was captivating to watch, and her jumps were executed with precision. Her body was flexible enough to enable her to perform spins of the highest calibre at the fastest speed. Her personality and skillset were now looking promising enough for her to gain a scholarship in America for the following summer.

However, her coach was neglecting to address her mental health and wellbeing. Her methods were questionable, with only one thing on her mind: for Vanessa to become an

Olympic Champion. She was unaware of the psychological damage she was doing in the process. Vanessa's anxiety and low self-esteem were spiralling out of control through lack of praise and positive feedback. Her coach was always telling her that, when she was her age, she'd been performing at a much higher level. This left Vanessa continually questioning herself, and her joy and enthusiasm for skating was beginning to wane.

Vanessa began to lose trust in her coach. She was never satisfied with anything she did on the ice, often shouting at her when she felt that a manoeuvre wasn't perfect. She persistently interrupted her during her programmes to tell her that she'd done something wrong. She created drama out of nowhere, and Vanessa despised her negativity. But whenever Vanessa tried to speak to her about it, she didn't want to listen.

By now, she had reached a critical point where she was no longer putting in sufficient effort, because she believed it to be fruitless. She was filled with guilt and shame, because she was unable to please her coach. This made her feel frustrated because she had always worked so hard in the past.

Peering through her bedroom window, Vanessa was disappointed that there was no snow, but instead the sun shone brightly in the cloudless sky. The freezing cold winter was upon them, and the amber and red weather warnings for a thick blanket of snow had proven wrong.

So now there was no excuse. She would have to go to her skating lesson. She still hadn't been selected for the American scholarship, but she wasn't even sure if she cared any longer.

She'd asked her mother if she could change to a different coach, but no one else could teach to the standard she needed. Juliet who was Rochelle's coach had refused to take her on, because she believed it would disrupt Rochelle's lessons.

Rochelle's recent progress had not gone unnoticed by Vanessa. Although she had gone through a patch of not enjoying her skating, she had bounced back, and now had more of the energy Vanessa so envied about her. She never seemed to give up, and her hopes for an Olympic gold had not been dashed. She was also in the running for a scholarship in America, but there were only two places available for figure skaters from England.

Both of the girls were skating for longer periods now. Friday afternoons were no longer spent in school, as they had acquired special permission to skate instead. So, for both of them, their entire weekends were spent at the rink.

But Vanessa had begun to question why she'd wanted to be an Olympic skater in the first place. Was it even an achievable goal? Was she still certain that this was what she wanted? Why was she so negative and frustrated with herself? Where had the fire in her belly gone?

She blew on her bedroom window and, in the icy steam, she wrote, '*Vanessa sucks!*'

But she actually knew the answers to all of her questions. It wasn't the skating that she despised; it was her coach. She had affected her self-esteem.

She suddenly realised that her goal was achievable. She just had to believe in herself. All she needed to do was to remain focused on herself and to be aware that her coach was an impatient, ambitious and aggressive woman. She must remember that it was a personality trait, and that it wasn't aimed personally at Vanessa.

Feeling more positive than she had in a long time, she realised that all she needed to do was to begin enjoying her skating again, and to ignore the nagging by her coach.

As her mother drove her to the rink, she couldn't wait to get there and put her skates on. She had direction again: an ultimate goal to aim for. It didn't matter about her coach's issues. She'd rediscovered her own moral value of herself.. All her fears, useless worry and uneasiness had lifted.

Feeling proud of herself, she leant across to her mother and kissed her on the cheek. Her dream was alive again.

"I love you! Thanks for giving up so much of your time and money to enable me to skate," she whispered.

CHAPTER 14

Rochelle sat in her bedroom trying to resolve some of the issues she was experiencing due to the traumatic loss of her parents, and the damage done to her at the children's home. She was anxious, traumatised, insecure and jealous, resulting from the abuse and manipulation she'd experienced in the past. She was riddled with hurt and rejection. She was worried that Derek and Gloria's love for her might not last. Although her friendship with Vanessa had improved again of late, she still felt isolated and vulnerable. When she skated her worries faded away, but as soon as she was back home, or at school, they again overwhelmed her.

A tear crossed her cheek as a rush of sadness gripped her deep within. An urge to run overcame her. She grabbed her trainers and headed for the front door.

"Mum, I'm going for a run," she shouted.

As she raced along the driveway and into the street, she became exhilarated as her horrible thoughts and emotions floated away. She imagined herself soaring high like an eagle, full of power. As the saying goes, she felt as free as a bird. She told herself that she was beautiful, brave, courageous, proud, determined and graceful, all of which she experienced when she skated. She would never surrender to those awful emotions again. She would be strong. She would fight to win the Olympic gold medal. She would protect herself from pain and would be fearless. She would complete her dream by remaining focused, and would make sure she won the scholarship to America. She would take on the challenge. She was unique. She would not run away from anything, other than those negative thoughts. She would make everyone love and adore her. She would never give up. This would be her life from now on. Her real parents would be proud of her if they could see her now.

She laughed out loud to herself; she was happy.

And so it was that she earned herself the nickname of 'The Bulldog'. Everyone around her noticed her new, fighting mental attitude to life, her mysterious concrete tenacity, and how she stayed grounded as her serious and self-contained demeanour became positive, kinder and gentler. She was self-sufficient, determined and was becoming more and more independent. Her confidence grew and she found ways to solve her awkward behavioural problems without needing the guidance of others.

CHAPTER 15

"I don't want to see it! I don't want to know what I've done!" Rochelle cried, en route to the hospital. She couldn't move her right wrist without it causing her to scream out in agony.

She'd been attempting to land a triple salchow during a training session when she'd landed in an awkward position, and her right wrist had taken the full force of the fall.

Tears cascaded down her cheeks as the hospital doctor explained that her wrist was shattered. She heaved as if she was going to vomit as she glanced at her hand, which was pointing in a contrasting direction to her arm. Her dream of gaining the scholarship to America was as shattered as her wrist.

Vanessa had seen the fall and heard her screams. She knew straight away the scholarship was now hers for the taking, but she wasn't elated; instead, she was sad for Rochelle. There had only ever been two scholarships available, and she'd always hoped that she and Rochelle would both win one of them.

The drive home from the hospital was a long one for Rochelle, her arm now encased in a white plaster cast. The doctor had told her she wouldn't be able to skate for at least six weeks, or maybe even longer.

She stared out of the car's rear window in silence, having told Derek and Gloria that she didn't want to talk about what had happened. She watched the endless white lines on the tarmac; this was how her life was going to be in the future … endless and boring. The green fields at the side of the motorway held no pleasure for her either. There was to be no more pleasure for her. Everything was depressing, even the trees they passed. What was the purpose of trees? What was the purpose of her?

She looked upwards at the dark, grey clouds and realised that her mood was as dark and grey as they were. As they threatened to spill into rain, her mood threatened to spill into tears. The humdrum sound of the car engine was like the humdrum of her life, ticking over, moving forward but not getting anywhere. She lifted her arm to her face and sniffed the plaster cast. It smelled chalky and reminded her of the caves they had visited on their camping trip when she was a little girl. She studied the backs of Derek and Gloria's heads. What were they thinking? Did they regret adopting her?

Gloria broke the silence.

"I know you don't want to talk about it, Rochelle, but I can't stand this atmosphere any longer. We've been in the car for over an hour now, and nobody's said a single word. We'll still be able to do things, you know. You'll still be able to go to school. And we can go out for nice walks together."

Derek interjected, glancing through the rear-view mirror.

"You'll have more time for reading, too. You used to love your books, and I haven't seen you with one in ages."

"I'm not sure how I would even hold a book and turn the pages," she whined. "And as for school, how am I going to be able to write when I'm right-handed? I've blown the scholarship, too. I'll be so unfit by the time I get back into training."

"Your brain is reacting like a cluster bomb, causing you to panic. You just need to give your wrist time to heal, that's all. As for your fitness, yes, you may lose muscle tone, but it will come back as soon as you start training again, especially at your age."

Gloria tried to console her. She leaned into the back of the car to pat Rochelle's knee comfortingly.

"You'll be able to watch more TV, and you'll have more time to study. You can use this time to get on top of your school work, too," Derek added.

"I'll lose touch with Vanessa. She'll definitely be going off to America for the summer now, and I won't be," she sobbed. "Anyway, I don't want to talk anymore."

The same infinite sadness she'd previously experienced was resurfacing. Once again, everything seemed pointless. It was as if the world was against her. She closed her eyes to try and shut it all out.

A week later, Rochelle found herself sitting opposite a lady who was to become her counsellor, Gloria and Derek having become so concerned about her eating and sleeping habits, and her refusal to participate in anything.

The lady introduced herself,

"I'm Kathy, and I'm here to try and help you with the upsetting feelings and emotions you've been suffering from lately. It's good to meet you, Rochelle."

"I don't know what to say," Rochelle replied. "I sort of want to be here, and I sort of don't. I know I don't want to feel this way anymore. I was getting better. I was so happy, but after breaking my wrist, it was as if I was four years old again, and had just been told that my parents were never coming back."

She studied the carpet.

"Well, today we are going to discuss gratitude and the meaning behind the word ... what it means to both of us. So, I'll go first.

"For me, heartfelt gratitude is essential for happiness. It's a state of mind, which thrives when we possess internal peace. So, tell me. What does it mean to you, Rochelle?"

"It means you appreciate everything you have in life, and are satisfied with it, I guess."

She glanced up at Kathy.

"That's right, Rochelle. If you're not grateful, the things you already have won't matter to you. You're always going to be looking for something more."

"I know that, but my dream is to be an Olympic skater."

She rubbed the fingers of her left-hand over the plaster cast.

"I understand it's difficult for you not to resent the fact that your real parents were killed when you were so young. But you could show gratitude to your adoptive parents, because they love you, and it was you they chose to shower their love upon."

"So, does that mean I'm meant to show them gratitude for what they've given me, and forget about what I could have had with my real parents?"

Rochelle fidgeted uncomfortably in her chair.

"Yes! You've found the strength to come through the loss of your parents, and I'm sure you're strong enough to overcome this hurdle, too."

"But my whole future is now in question!

Everything I've ever dreamed of!"

She glared at Kathy.

"It's understandable for you to be angry and upset, but it won't help you in the long term."

"I want to know more about my parents' deaths and the accident. Everyone was so secretive at the time. Nobody wanted to talk about it, and because I had no living relatives, there was never anyone to ask about it."

She gulped for air. The room suddenly felt hot and stuffy.

"I know you want to get back into training as soon as you can, Rochelle, but this break from it may do you some good. It will give you time to focus on resolving some of your issues."

"I *am* sad, but I'm grateful to Derek and Gloria, too."

The hint of a smile crossed her face.

"Before I see you next week, I want you to write down in a notebook every positive experience you have during the week."

"My head is so foggy at the moment. My mind is so unclear."

She placed her left hand on her forehead.

"It's understandable, considering everything that's happened to you from such a young age. Don't give yourself such a hard time of it. You need to ask yourself what is useful to you here."

"I try to be kind to Derek and Gloria, and to my best friend Vanessa, but sometimes I get it all wrong," she frowned.

"When your sleeping pattern is no longer disturbed and you're eating three square meals again, you will feel a lot less fragile. I'm going to give you a meditation CD to help you become more comfortable with falling asleep at night. You can listen to it in the daytime as well, if you find it helps."

"Thank you. I get so anxious and overwhelmed at times."

She stared out of the window.

"I also want you to take a daily walk, either by yourself or with Gloria, depending on whether you want to spend time alone or in the company of someone else."

"I enjoy running … but I'm not allowed to at the moment."

She lifted up her arm and pointed at her plaster cast.

"I get scared that something bad will happen to Derek and Gloria. They might get killed in a terrible accident, or decide they don't want me to live with them anymore."

CHAPTER 16

Rochelle turned 15. Her wrist had made a full recovery, and she was training again, albeit at a slower pace. She didn't mind, as tonight she couldn't sleep. But it wasn't through worry, it was excitement. She was sure she'd fallen in love. She was exhilarated and euphoric. She couldn't stop daydreaming about him. The object of her desires was Lloyd Varley, who was two years above her at school.

Propped up in bed with her laptop open, she was talking to him on FaceTime, the blue haze from the screen lighting up her face in her darkened bedroom.

"She won't let me go that far by train. I'd have to lie, and I don't particularly want to upset her and end up in a load of trouble. Can't we meet somewhere closer? Leeds is too far for me to get away with it."

"You need to stand your ground. Fifteen, aren't you, now?" he flashed a perfect smile.

"Yeah, but I'm not seventeen, like you. I can't just do as I please."

"What are they? Catholics or something? Keep you shut away like a nun?"

Again, his perfect grin lit up her screen.

She laughed as she drooled over him. He was everything she wanted: sophisticated, clever, sharp-tongued, well-dressed and street-wise. She liked his pale skin and fair hair, which curled in its scruffy manner. His well-spoken, deep voice sent shivers down her spine.

She'd met him in the park after school one day, and he'd told her that he fancied her. She'd giggled in response, and he'd told her she'd reacted that way because she was only 15. There'd been a silence as she'd looked into his eyes, and before she knew what was happening, he'd kissed her fully on the lips. That was the moment she'd been sure she'd fallen in love.

He'd asked her to go to the beach by the lake with him, but she'd told him that she had to be home by six at the latest. He'd said it wasn't a problem as he could go back to hers with her. Her face blushing, she'd explained that Gloria and Derek would throw a fit. He'd remained silent, kissed her again and had left her standing there in a daze, the sun shining brighter than she had ever noticed before.

"They're not my real parents. I'm adopted," she explained, giving him the prettiest smile she could via her inexpensive laptop.

"Does that mean they can even tell you what you can and can't do?"

"Of course! They're my Mum and Dad now. My own parents were killed in a car crash when I was four."

She propped herself higher up against the pillow.

Lloyd smiled at her.

"I'm sorry! That's awful! I didn't know that about you. So, is Erickson your real name, or your adoptive parents' name?"

"It's my real parents' surname. I chose to keep it, and Derek and Gloria are fine with it."

She frowned a little. Her anxiety was rising, and her chest had tightened. Why had she told him she was adopted, when nobody else at her senior school, other than Vanessa, knew about it. In fact, the only person she had told since leaving junior school was Vanessa.

"I wish I could hug you right now, Rochelle. You look like you need a hug."

He leant forwards, nearer to his screen.

Her body shook, wishing that he could give her a protective hug right now.

"I wish you could, too," she smiled.

This strong, good-looking boy was exactly what she'd dreamed of … her own boyfriend. She wouldn't be jealous any longer of the other girls at school who already had boyfriends.

"Rochelle! Who are you talking to at this time of night?"

Gloria opened her bedroom door, as Rochelle snapped her laptop shut.

"Can't you learn to knock? I was reciting the words for the school play."

The lie was out of her mouth before she could stop herself. She fluffed up her pillow and lay down.

"It's quite late. You should be asleep by now."

As the weeks went by, Rochelle's relationship with Lloyd had developed. She loved the way he seemed to understand her, like nobody else had before, not even Vanessa. He seemed to know exactly what to say to help her whenever she was upset. He would drop everything if she needed or wanted to see him. They spent as much time together as possible, talking about what they'd been doing when they were apart. They shared their feelings, and they understood each other's point of view. As time went on, she felt less vulnerable around him. The mutual trust they had for each other grew deeper with each passing day, as did their affection. There was a special bond between them. She hung on his every word, wanting to learn more and more about him.

They often went to the cinema together, and would sit and talk about the films in great detail afterwards. He told her about his own personal and academic issues. They had still only hugged and kissed, him holding her gently in his arms, and Rochelle was happy that he hadn't tried to pressurise her into doing anything further than that.

Lloyd's amusing sense of humour set him

apart from anyone else she had ever known. He never ran out of jokes. She found his observations about other people hysterical, and some of the pranks he pulled made her laugh out loud.

Today, they had met in the park, after she had hurried out of school. As soon as she spotted him, she ran towards him in her three-inch high heels – the highest that school regulations allowed. He still had to tilt his head downwards in order to meet her parted lips with his own. The rain cascaded from the sky, but neither of them cared as they held each other's hand and headed towards the nearby shelter of the trees.

"When are you going to tell Derek and Gloria about me? Are you embarrassed? I'm fed up having to sneak around like this all the time."

"I'm worried they'll stop me from seeing you," she said, kicking at the ground.

Lloyd ran his finger over his upper lip.

"Are you sure that's all it is?"

"Well, it's the age thing, too: me being only 15, and you 17. I know they won't approve."

She ducked under the low-hanging branch of a tree.

One of the boys from Lloyd's class walked by, and Lloyd dropped his hand from Rochelle's.

"Hi, Nick! How're you doing, mate? Might see you later ... play some football ... if it ever stops pissing with rain."

As Nick disappeared out of sight, Rochelle said, "See! It's no different the other way around. You don't want the boys in your year knowing you're dating me either."

Lloyd bit his lip. She was right. He hadn't wanted to flaunt her in front of his mates, nor his whole catastrophic family. Although his violent, alcoholic parents knew he had a girlfriend, he hadn't told them she was only 15. Also, he had hidden his poor background from Rochelle. She didn't know he lived in one of the grim houses on the rough council estate, as the kids in school described it. He had lied to her and told her he lived in one of the fairy-tale cottages on the small path by the lake. Maybe it was best he hadn't pushed to meet her parents. By the sound of it, he would never be good enough for her in their eyes. She may not even want him herself, if she saw the state of his own poor home.

"I sometimes wish I was you, Rochelle, with your dreams and aspirations. I dunno what I want from life, or where my life's even going."

He pulled a leaf from the tree. Rochelle kissed him on the cheek.

"It'll come to you. I've got every confidence in you."

"You're so kind, I don't deserve you," he said, stroking her cheek.

She laughed.

"Don't be silly!"

She squeezed his hand, surprised by his comment. She believed it to be the reverse – that she didn't deserve him."

A creeping sense of unease gripped them both at the same time. Maybe their age difference did matter? For Rochelle, the sweet magic of their blossoming relationship had just turned a little sour, and the park had lost some of its beauty.

"I love you," he said.

"I love you, too," she replied. But she was uncertain about her feelings, and she turned her head away from him.

By now, Rochelle had become used to her counselling sessions with Kathy, and they greeted each other with smiles as Rochelle entered the counsellor's familiar, white-walled room.

"So how have you been this week?" Kathy opened, adjusting herself in her chair. "How many days have you had where you've taken little interest or pleasurc in doing things?"

"None at all," she replied "I'm on top of the world."

"That's great, Rochelle. That's music to my ears. How has your sleeping pattern been?"

She leaned slightly forward.

"Good!"

"Have you been tired or lacking in energy?"

She stood up and poured them both a glass of water from the jug on the table at the other side of the room.

"No! I've been fine."

"And eating – your appetite? How has that been?"

She handed one of the glasses to Rochelle.

"All good! I'm putting on weight."

"Have you experienced any negative thoughts about yourself?"

Kathy settled back into her chair and took a sip of water.

Rochelle studied the red carpet on the floor for a couple of minutes, unable to meet Kathy's eyes.

"Well, no negative thoughts … but I *have* lied to Gloria and Derek."

"Why have you lied to them?"

She placed the glass on the table at her side.

Again, Rochelle studied the carpet.

Ashamed of herself, she replied, "I've lied to them loads. I've got a boyfriend and they don't know about him, so I've told them a pack of lies about where I've been going, and who I've been with."

"Why did you feel the need to lie to them?"

"Because they won't like him."

"Why wouldn't they like him? If you like him, why wouldn't they?"

She flicked back a piece of hair from her face.

"He's older than me. Two years older."

Kathy smiled.

"That's no reason for them not to like him, especially if he's a nice boy. Try them out, they might surprise you."

"I'm scared they'll stop me from seeing him," Rochelle replied, hugging her knees to her chest.

"I'm sure they will, if they catch you lying to them. They'll think you have something to hide. But if you told them and they accepted him, wouldn't it be nice not to have to tell lies and sneak around? Wouldn't it make you less anxious and on edge about him? It must be a big worry for you that you'll get found out. You'd be more relaxed in your relationship with him, too."

An alarm sounded to indicate the session was over.

The following morning, Rochelle got up filled with hope and enthusiasm about telling Gloria and Derek about Lloyd. Nothing was going to stand in her way; she was definitely going to tell them.

As she brushed and braided her hair into a thick golden rope, she smiled at herself in the mirror, and her heart leapt with joy. Her hopes and dreams were back on track. One day she would be an Olympic skater, with a gorgeous boyfriend who loved her, and a loving Mum and Dad who cared about her.

At the breakfast table in the kitchen, she initiated the conversation.

"Mum, Dad, I've got something to tell you. I've been scared to tell you, and I'm sorry, but I've lied to you as well. I spoke to Kathy about it yesterday, and she said it's best to tell you. I've got a boyfriend."

Derek couldn't hide his anger.

"You've been lying to us? For how long? Fifteen! You're fifteen! You don't need a boyfriend at your age!"

"Calm down, Derek. Hear her out. Why did you lie to us, Rochelle?" Gloria asked, leaning over to pat her on her arm.

"Because I knew this is how you'd react. Why are you so angry, Dad?"

"It's fine, Rochelle. I'm not angry, I'm just shocked," he said taking a sip of tea.

Rochelle glared at him. His expression was that of someone who was trying to understand … Rochelle called it his headmaster's face. She believed that he was playing headmaster now, not her caring Dad. She knew that whatever she said, he would pretend that he cared, but his anger showed in his eyes.

Her resentment was boiling over. She moved the spoon around in her empty breakfast bowl, refusing to look at his serious face.

Little did she know, but he was actually admiring her honesty, and thinking how beautiful she was. All he wanted was for her to lead an uncomplicated and happy life.

She pushed her chair back from the breakfast table and scurried into the hallway. She grabbed her heavy school bag and slammed the front door behind her.

She phoned Lloyd.

"Can you meet me in the park before school? I've left the house early."

"Yeah, sure! You okay?"

"No! But I'll explain when I see you."

She switched off her phone as she walked briskly towards the bus stop.

CHAPTER 17

Rochelle met Vanessa for breakfast at the rink café.

"I'm so lucky to have you as a friend, Vanessa. I believe you and Lloyd came into my life for a reason. But I can't understand why Gloria and Derek wouldn't allow me to date him until I turned 16. They can be so old-fashioned at times."

"Well, I guess they care about you, and with him being two years older, they were just trying to protect you."

"I know, but it wasn't an easy time for me. I was so angry with them."

Rochelle's eyes glazed over.

"I do love him, you know. He took it all so well and said he would wait."

"I've always got your back too, you know, Rochelle. I'll always look out for you. And I'm sure you'll do the same for me."

Rochelle hugged Vanessa.

"Besties forever! Now, let's get on the ice and get some practice in."

The moment Rochelle's well-worn skates made contact with the ice, the blissful sense of flying with the eagles took her away into her other magical world. As she glided across the ice, her mind turned to Lloyd and how excited she was about seeing him for bonfire night the following day. It was a time of year that always helped to burn away any anger and frustrations she was feeling.

It was to be their first proper date since she'd turned 16. They'd seen each other for short periods at the park, and had chatted for hours over FaceTime, but they had respectfully stuck to Gloria and Derek's rules. In fact, with Rochelle's hectic skating schedule, she'd had very little free time, anyway.

She loved the autumn: the glorious colours of the trees and the crisp, autumnal air. But, best of all, she loved bonfire night: the smell of bonfire smoke, grilled sausages, fat, juicy burgers and fried onions.

Her thoughts returned to her skating. She still dreamed of the ultimate test of her abilities: the Olympics. She visualised herself and Vanessa beaming at one another whilst they stood proudly on the podium as the national anthem was blaring out, she with the gold medal hanging around her neck and Vanessa sporting the silver one. One magnificent moment! One mutual lifelong dream!

She would train harder, with more energy, until she would explode onto the ice on that momentous day, revealing her full potential for the entire world to admire.

She landed a little precariously after a particularly challenging jump, and an all-too-familiar sense of doubt crept into her mind. She knew she needed to lose her emotional baggage, so she pushed the introspection away. Negative analysis would not make her a champion.

Her sombre thoughts were broken as she spotted Gloria beckoning to her from the side of the rink.

What was Gloria doing there? Was something wrong? She raced over to her.

"What's the matter? What are you doing here at the rink? Has something happened to Derek?"

Gloria put her arm around her and led her to a private area at the back of the rink.

"Come and sit over here. It's not Derek. It's Lloyd. I'm afraid he was involved in an accident this morning on his way to work. A car hit him as he was crossing the road.

"I'm so sorry, Rochelle, but he didn't make it. They tried to save him, but it was too late. They couldn't do anything for him ..."

Her world fell apart!

Her sense of security vanished!

Her mind rushed back to her parents' accident. It was as though it was happening all over again.

She would never again be able to tell Lloyd that she loved him. All their dreams of a future together were shattered. It made no sense! How could this have happened? She couldn't comprehend it.

She'd had no chance to say goodbye to her parents, and now she couldn't say goodbye to Lloyd either.

She hated this world! Why was everyone she loved snatched away from her with no warning? Who would be next? Was it all because of her?

The world had once more become a frightening, unpredictable place – a place she didn't want to be part of. All of the scars from her parents' deaths opened up. She realised that tomorrow was promised to no one, and she didn't want it to be promised to her.

Lloyd's funeral came and went. She thought about going to visit his parents, but as she'd never met them, she decided it probably wasn't a good idea. The day of his funeral, she locked herself away in her bedroom to grieve privately for her love that never truly was. How could she show up at the funeral, when his family didn't even know who she was? They would just think she was some stupid, young girl who was bawling her eyes out over someone she barely knew.

She sat on her bed and wrote them a letter, but she couldn't find the right words, so she screwed it up and threw it in her bin.

A couple of weeks later, she found herself

sitting opposite Kathy again, all of their previous counselling sessions having been utterly undone.

"I'm so sorry, Rochelle," Kathy said, shifting uncomfortably in her chair.

"Oh, Kathy! I feel so empty! I'm so alone, and I have a hollow, aching feeling inside me. Losing Lloyd is so raw, but what's worse is, it's opened up all of the memories I have of my parents. I don't want to live any longer. It's strange though, the tears won't come. It's as if I have no soul."

"It's okay to be sad, Rochelle. I would be far more worried if you weren't," she said with an apologetic smile.

"Can't you make it all go away? That's what you're paid for, isn't it? … to help me feel okay?"

"It's going to hurt like hell for a while, Rochelle. Another tragic door has opened in your life, and it will never be fully closed again."

"I'm so angry with Derek and Gloria for stopping me from seeing him for so long. All that time we could have spent together. I bet nobody stopped *them* from dating when *they* were young. Why did they put stupid boundaries in place? They never made him feel comfortable, even after I turned 16. All they ever went on about was sex, as if it was the only thing Lloyd ever wanted from me. Don't they think we had any respect for each other?"

"Have you been eating properly, Rochelle? You look as though you've lost a bit of weight?"

"Well, at least it's one bonus! No, I haven't! I've no appetite."

She stood up.

"I'm done here," she yelled, "and this isn't helping. It's a waste of time. I'll sort it out in my own way."

She tossed her thick, blonde hair to one side and walked out, slamming the heavy, grey door behind her, its colour reflecting her mood.

She walked towards home at the slowest pace possible, kicking at the pebbles along the difficult, stony path, wishing it was her own beautiful Mum and caring Dad who'd be greeting her when she got back … not stupid Derek and Gloria.

Her thoughts drifted as she walked along.

She daydreamed about whether she would have had brothers or sisters if they had lived. She thought about school. She hadn't been there since Lloyd's accident, and she had no intention of going back. Derek and Gloria and their pathetic, conservative outlook! She missed her chats with Lloyd about the pros and cons of socialism. Okay, he was working in a charity shop, but it didn't mean that Derek and Gloria could look down their snobbish noses at him. It had only been a temporary job, anyway. He would have gone on to bigger and better things. But now, he would never be able to prove himself to them. Yes, his family were poor, but Derek and Gloria weren't that rich themselves!

Almighty God! She hated Him! Did He even exist? And, if He did exist, why would He be so cruel?

She thought about her skating. She hadn't been to the rink since Lloyd's accident. Maybe it was time to go back? … to focus on her primary goal? But she wasn't sure she could face it. Everyone at the rink would know about it.

But, she couldn't throw it all away, could she? … maybe she could!

Vanessa had called her dozens of times since

it happened, and left her lots of voicemails. But she couldn't face speaking to her yet … although part of her desperately wanted to.

Her thoughts returned to Lloyd. If he'd lived, would they have got married? Would they have travelled the world together? She heard his kind laugh in her mind. She missed his laugh, and the way it had always cheered her up. He'd made her giggle so many times. Would she ever laugh that way again? … until her ribs hurt? Probably not!

She thumped a concrete wall with her fist as she walked past it, scowling with a deepening sense of anger. There was no joy left to make her heart leap … no more pleasure to be had. Her future was now lined with a fear – a fear that made her heart pump and beat like it was trying to escape. She could never love again! Would she ever be able to forgive Derek and Gloria for not allowing her to spend more time with Lloyd?

A small, balding man walked towards her, pulling a spaniel on a lead. The dog sniffed at her trouser leg. She bent over and patted its silky, brown head. A torrent of tears overcame her. The spaniel had found her weak spot and exposed it.

She kicked a particularly big stone and told

herself to snap out of her negative mood. She rushed along the twisting path at break-neck speed, wanting to get home as soon as possible.

Gloria was waiting in the hallway looking anxious. Kathy must have called her to say she'd walked out of her counselling session. Gloria handed her a box of chocolates.

"These might help to cheer you up a little, my love."

"Thanks, Mum," she said, and snatched the box from her hand. Upstairs in her room, she devoured the whole box.

She couldn't sleep. In fact, she hadn't slept properly since the accident.

She wanted to call Vanessa. She wanted to tell her that she wanted to go back to skating but she was too embarrassed.

What would she say to her? *"Don't get close to me, or else you might die!"*

She curled herself up into the foetus position, pulled the thick, blue duvet over her head and sobbed herself to sleep.

The crying did her good. She slept well and woke the next morning to the smell of baking bread. It drew her downstairs to the kitchen. Her appetite was returning.

"Hi, Mum. Can I have a bacon sandwich when the bread's ready?"

Gloria gave her an approving smile.

"Of course, you can, my love. You're looking a little perkier. Did you get a better night's sleep?"

"Yeah! I did, actually. I didn't wake once. My dreams were better than reality. I'm going to call Vanessa this morning and ask her to go to the rink with me for some impromptu practice."

"That's great news, Rochelle," Gloria said.

She leant over and gave her a motherly kiss on her pale cheek.

"Derek and I love you so much, you know. We've been so worried about you. We thought Lloyd's death might be the final straw for you."

"Well, let's not get ahead of ourselves. I'm only going skating," she said, pulling out a chair from the breakfast table.

Vanessa was relieved to be back at the rink

with Rochelle. Her own skating had suffered as a consequence of the awful news she'd witnessed Rochelle react to from the safety of the ice. The scream that Rochelle had let out when Gloria had broken the news had pierced her nightmares ever since.

"I'm so pleased we're back on the ice, Rochelle. We can't have any distractions if we want to win those Olympic medals. Do you want to skate first, and I'll study your performance? Or shall we do it the other way around?"

Rochelle went first. Vanessa was shocked by how below par she skated. Her heart didn't seem to be in the performance at all; it was bland. She executed all of her moves without any obvious errors, but there was no soul there. It was as if something had died inside her.

As she came off the ice, Vanessa lied to her friend, wanting to encourage her.

"It was great! Your style was outstanding."

"Don't lie, Vanessa! It was awful! I feel just like the weather outside: dull and grey, with no sun shining through."

Vanessa winced. It looked like the Olympic gold medal would be hers at this rate, but it didn't make her happy. She needed her friend to drive her forwards. The competition between them was what had always motivated her to improve her own skating. Would Rochelle ever get her mojo back? Vanessa wasn't so sure.

"Your life was never going to be filled with rainbows and unicorns, was it, Rochelle! It's so unfair how much has already been thrown at you, and you're still only 16. Your skating is bound to be affected for a while, but I'm convinced you'll come out of this stronger than before. You'll skate with great passion, and you'll do it for your real parents, and for Lloyd. I just know it."

She placed her arm around Rochelle's shoulders.

"Spare me the tedious lecture, Vanessa! I was crap and I'm always gonna be crap. I'm never gonna get over this. I may as well give up now!"

Despite the last one not having gone well, Gloria persuaded Rochelle to continue with her counselling sessions. In the end, as low as she was feeling, Rochelle agreed that it couldn't make her any worse. So, on the day after the dreadful skating session with Vanessa, she found herself back in Kathy's office.

"It's good to see you, Rochelle. I want to start by explaining the emotions you've been experiencing. They're normal and healthy reactions to what you've experienced. There will be a range of emotions like sadness, resentfulness, paranoia, numbness, an inability to calm yourself, a yearning, shock, hopelessness, fear, loneliness and guilt. These are all normal reactions to such a loss."

"My brain seems to have slowed down, I've lost all trust and my dreams are shattered."

"The sorrowful casket of grief is cruel and shows up in many different forms, Rochelle."

"I'm never going to be able to love again."

"You will, but at present you are naturally trying to find a way to protect yourself."

"I'm so numb."

"Have you experienced any positive emotions since Lloyd's death?"

"No."

"Sadly, you've experienced so much loss in your short life."

"But, my skating was crap."

"What sort of emotion did you experience while you were performing?"

"I felt dull and grey … as though there was no such thing as sunshine. My body felt heavy."

"People believe that grief is something we need to fix, heal or cure. I don't see it in that way. I see it as a natural and healthy reaction."

"I'm scared that I'm never gonna fix."

"You're more resilient and resourceful than you think, Rochelle."

"I just want it all to end."

Kathy handed her a tissue.

"It's okay to let the tears spill out. Don't hold them in."

"I feel like everything is out of control. I'm trapped and afraid, like I'm choking."

"How are Gloria and Derek responding to Lloyd's death?"

"They're trying to help me, but they don't know how to."

"I know you prefer being tucked away in your bedroom, but I'd like you to try and socialise."

"The minute I leave my room, I become even more stressed."

"Who do you feel safe around?"

"Nobody! Not even Vanessa. I'm not even sure I want to carry on with my skating at the moment. But part of me knows I'd miss it. Vanessa is tough. I have the utmost respect for her. Her skating is so impressive. She's going to achieve remarkable results.

"Part of me still wants to compete with her – to push us both forward – but she's a different character to me. She's not had all the knock-backs in her life like I have. She's not afraid to take risks in her skating. If I go back, it will be so freaking tough. She's going to be difficult to beat.

"I wish I could rise above all this. I used to be so dedicated to my skating; it gave my life meaning and purpose. I've put so much time and energy into it, and now I'm feeling so weak. I feel as though I'll never reap from what I've sown. It's as if a knife has cut straight through to my core. I feel destroyed. I need some space, away from it all."

The following morning was bright and blustery. Rochelle's brain stuttered for a moment as she answered a loud knock at the front door and found Vanessa standing there. They never usually showed up at each other's houses. Any spare time they had was spent practising at the rink.

"Well, are you gonna invite me in? Or are you just gonna stand there gawping at me?" she said, one foot already through the doorway.

"Yeah! Sorry! Come on in! You took me by surprise, that's all."

Rochelle was glad that Derek and Gloria were both at work, and she and Vanessa could have a private conversation. She knew that if Gloria had been home, she would have tried to eavesdrop on their chat, even if she'd taken Vanessa up to her bedroom.

Rochelle led her friend into the sitting room.

"Are you okay? How come you're not at the rink?" she asked.

"I wanted to see you. I'm hurting 'cos you're hurting. If I can't fix you, I can't fix me!"

"To be honest, I'm beyond fixing," Rochelle said, flopping onto to the sofa.

"You're stronger than you think, Rochelle. You know you can bounce back from this, right?"

"I'm sorry, Vanessa. I'm not the person you believe I am."

"But I don't want you to hurt anymore. I'll do anything I can to help you."

"I know! I don't wanna waste my life, but I'm so unhappy," she said as a tear rolled down her cheek.

"I know time is precious, I know this more than most people."

Vanessa leaned forward and clasped Rochelle's trembling hand in her own.

"You know I care about you so much, don't you?"

" Thank you, I know you do."

"Well, I never want to lose you. You're my best friend."

CHAPTER 18

Everything had changed! Rochelle's life would never be the same again. Her outlook on life had changed. Lloyd's death had wreaked devastation on her soul.

However, a year later life went on, but Rochelle had changed so much. To a certain extent, skating filled the void that Lloyd had left behind, but it didn't heal *all* of her wounds. Her skating gave her a modicum of freedom, and a slim sense of hope. She was even more determined to win the Olympic gold, and her extra effort was delivering dramatic improvements. Her energy and ambition were driven by her dreams of winning the medal for Lloyd and her real parents.

Her pain was still there. But she stuck rigidly to her skating schedule, putting on a brave face, even when she didn't feel up to it.

Beneath the surface, though, she still carried an element of fear and unease. She didn't trust life. Lloyd's death seemed so pointless. What's more, she no longer felt that Derek and Gloria were her Mum and Dad. She hadn't forgiven them for how they had treated Lloyd. They'd become strangers, even though deep down she knew that she was scared to love them for fear of losing them.

Vanessa stood by her every step of the way, sharing and understanding Rochelle's mood swings. Their connection was as strong as ever; if they weren't on the ice together, they were text messaging each other. They often shared private jokes, and Rochelle liked the way Vanessa was straight with her and pulled her up whenever she felt it was called for. She pointed out her blind spots, pushing her forward on the road to success and keeping her on the straight and narrow. She showed her how to use self-control to curb her tendency to sabotage her life.

Despite all of Vanessa's efforts, though, Rochelle had been keeping a little secret from everyone. She was binge eating. At any opportunity, she would rush to the local McDonald's, order two Big Macs and wolf them down as quickly as she could. Sometimes, she would treat herself to a family-size carton of ice cream and hide herself away in her bedroom until the last spoonful had been devoured. Her favourite midnight snack was a jar of Nutella. Occasionally, if Derek and Gloria were out, she would order a delivery of two large pizzas, and then eat the lot before they got home. Whenever this happened, guilt would overcome her, and she would punish herself by going for a five-mile run. By the same token, as a way of counterbalancing her binges, she would control some days' intake to just 1,000 calories.

Today was a controlled-diet day. Rochelle entered the rink and was greeted by Vanessa who made her giggle by giving her a goofy smile.

"Let's have a bit of fun, shall we, Rochelle? I'll skate and you can mirror all my moves."

"Yeah! Fine! But don't get showing off too much. I don't want to look ridiculous."

Within a couple of minutes, they were both laying on the ice in stitches of happy laughter. Vanessa had taken a fall, and Rochelle had copied her, landing in a heap on top of her friend.

At the end of their session, they rested on the side of the rink.

"I've got a secret, Rochelle," Vanessa announced. "I've met a boy. I hope you're okay with that … you know … having lost Lloyd. But I can't keep it from you any longer. I'm so excited."

She hopped from one foot to the other.

"Of course, I'm okay with it. It's about time! Seventeen and your first boyfriend! What's his name then, and where did you meet him?"

"Don't tell anyone, will you. I don't want anyone to know yet."

"Of course, I won't. Come on! Who is he? What's his name?"

Vanessa skated off laughing.

"I can't tell you, else I'd have to kill you."

Rochelle chased after her.

"When am I going to meet him?"

That night, Rochelle read herself to sleep,

but was woken in the middle of it by a sudden cold chill. As she opened her eyes in the darkness, she was sure she saw something move. She knew it was Lloyd.

He whispered in her ear.

"I love you, Rochelle. Go get that gold medal for me!"

She wrapped her arms around herself and imagined him kissing her, his lips brushing gently against hers. She hoped she'd never forget him. He'd been a wonderful kisser. Well, he *was* the only boy she'd ever kissed, so she had nothing to compare it with, but it had been so sensual and passionate.

The last weekend she'd spent with him had been wonderful. They'd spent most of the time kissing. She remembered how relaxed and loved he'd made her feel: secure and happy, at peace with herself. It was as if there would be no end to it all, but how wrong she'd been. She craved for more, but there would be no more.

She fell back to sleep, comforted by the knowledge that he was still there, even though it was only in spirit.

The following morning at the onset of daylight, the message Lloyd had whispered in her ear spurred her on. She would strive with all her heart to win the gold medal for him. She would surpass Vanessa, and all the other ambitious girls from all over the world. She would skate as if her life depended on it. The final victory would be hers. She would make no more stupid mistakes. She didn't always have to carry her pain and sadness around with her.

There would be no more binge eating. She would eat a healthy diet. She would break the bounds of her skating routine and take risks like Vanessa did. She would push herself out of her comfort zone. She couldn't afford to lose.

Vanessa watched from the side of the rink as Rochelle went through her programme. Her performance was sizzling. The old Rochelle was back. Rochelle spun, flexed and flew across the ice. The routine was impeccable.

Vanessa's excitement grew. The challenge was on!

"I knew you could do it, Rochelle. I just knew it."

Vanessa patted her friend on the back as she came off the ice.

"I said you'd bounce back. You're doing what Lloyd and your parents would have wanted you to do.

"Your life may have changed, but it was never ever over. You're going to be even better than you were before."

CHAPTER 19

The Winter Olympics were only a few months away. Rochelle and Vanessa could see the gold medal in their sights. A decade of training and competitions had brought them close to achieving their goals.

"It's gonna be emotional, Vanessa. I can't believe we're almost there."

"As long as we stay fit and healthy. It would be awful if one of us wasn't able to go, after all our hard work."

" It's going to be amazing," Rochelle said excitedly.

Rochelle's training had intensified over the last few months. She'd been skating every day from early morning until late at night. The energy around her was buzzing.

"I wonder what we'll do afterwards, though,

Rochelle? Do you think we'll both carry on skating?"

"I'm not sure! I want to do something more meaningful and beneficial with my life. Sure, I love skating but I want to venture out into the world … do more things."

"I'm glad I chose to skate. I don't have any regrets about it. I wouldn't change a thing."

"Have we been selfish, though? Derek and Gloria have had to sacrifice so many things to enable me to get this far. Has it all been worth it? What if we make a mess of it all and fail?"

"Well, we don't have a choice. We've come so far. We're flying high at the top of our sport now."

"I know, but I hate being in the press. I can't believe they printed an article about my parents' death and my adoption, I don't even know how they found out about it. My personal life printed all over the newspapers! It was awful for Derek and Gloria as well … everyone knowing I'm not their real daughter."

Vanessa skated off. She didn't want Rochelle to catch sight of the sly grin that had appeared on her face.

"I need to practise," she shouted back over her shoulder. "Catch you later."

She was sure Rochelle would never find out that she was the one who'd leaked the information about her private life. The competition was on, and she didn't intend to give the gold medal away to anyone, including Rochelle.

As Rochelle climbed the stairs that evening, she felt a sharp pain in her left knee. It was so bad that she had to shuffle up the top few stairs on her bottom. She must have overdone it. She was going to have to be a little more careful from now on.

She sat on her bed and rubbed some pain relief gel into her sore knee. As she did so, she mulled over how much her relationship with Vanessa had changed over the last few months. They never called or texted one another anymore, and the only conversations they had nowadays were brief ones at the rink. Vanessa had become hypercritical of Rochelle's skating, and she was more self-centred. Her kindness seemed to have disappeared, and her words were now often brutal. Gone was all the fun they'd had together in the past. She couldn't remember the last time they'd laughed together. Everything had become so serious. Their so-called 'unbreakable bond' had broken. Being around her was now uncomfortable for Rochelle.

She'd always known in her heart that there would be a price to pay to achieve her ultimate goal, but she hadn't expected it to cost her the friendship of her only true friend. She also knew that, if she was going to succeed, she needed to toughen up. She must forge ahead and ignore Vanessa's bitchiness, although part of her wished she could turn the clock back to when Vanessa had been so much kinder.

Overthinking was getting her nowhere, so she selected a meditation CD from the rack and placed it into her CD player. She was instantly at peace and drifted off into an exhausted sleep.

The following day, Rochelle's skating was affected by her feelings about Vanessa, and the bad blood running between them. She couldn't focus and began to speculate on how she could make it better.

"What's wrong with you today?" Juliet asked

her. "Your mind's not on it. You've lost your sparkle ."

"It's Vanessa. She's upsetting me. I don't know what I've done wrong, but she's so distant at the moment."

"Oh! Don't worry about her. Her ego's getting in the way. But it's her problem, not yours. She's getting way too big for those boots she's wearing. You've always been more talented than her anyway … even when you were both small."

"But, I don't know what I've done wrong."

"You haven't done anything wrong. She's just after the gold medal. She's using tactics … trying to unbalance you."

"Why would she? She's supposed to be my best friend."

"You can't allow her to have this effect on you, Rochelle. Trust me, it's affecting your performance. You're allowing her to win."

"But I'm so frustrated by it all. I'm trying not to let it get to me, but I can't help it."

The next couple of weeks became a living nightmare for Rochelle. Night and day, she was haunted by flashbacks of her parents' car accident and Lloyd's death. Her anxiety increased and her depression and anger issues resurfaced. Her mind had become confused once more, triggered by Vanessa's attitude towards her. Everything was out of control again, and she broke into sweats, with her heart racing and her breathing laboured.

As her bed awaited her at the end of another disastrous day, she placed a packet of paracetamol tablets on her bedside table.

Maybe she would take them or maybe she wouldn't?

Those pills could end all of my problems, she thought.

CHAPTER 20

The following week was a difficult one for Rochelle. She was in such a state. She just wanted to stay in bed all day. She spent most of her time crying and moping around.

Derek and Gloria were more worried than ever about her.

"What's up with you?" Gloria asked her. "You're only a couple of months away from the Olympics. Are you going to throw it all away? All your hard work up in smoke? All the money we've paid out, and the things we've gone without, for you to just sit around feeling sorry for yourself?"

"I know! I'm trying to snap out of it. But I never wanted to be a celebrity. I just wanted to be the best at my sport I could be. I can't stand seeing my name in the papers, and then there's all the hurtful stuff they're printing about Lloyd. Half of what they're printing, I didn't even know about, and I can't speak to him to find out what's true and what's not. It's as though everybody wants a part of me and I'm finding it difficult to come to terms with. I have no privacy. At least, here in my bedroom, I do."

"You need to focus on your skating, and forget about all of the other stuff."

"I know! I'm still confident I can win. I don't doubt my ability, but I need to get my head around this 'overnight celebrity' thing, or else I won't be able to deliver my best performance. I'm disappointed with Vanessa and how she's treating me, too. I just need some space to get over it all.

"For as long as I can remember, the gold medal is all I've dreamt of. I promise I'm not going to disappoint you, Mum, but I need this time to sort my head out, away from the public eye. The media attention has been so intense. Vanessa seems to be getting all the good press, but they seem to want to push me down a black hole."

"I'll come to the rink with you tomorrow … watch you train. I haven't been for a while. It'll be delightful to see you skate again."

"Thanks, Mum. It'll be comforting to know you're there. I need to put all these distractions behind me."

On the ice the following day, Rochelle pushed herself harder than ever. When she'd finished her routine, she smiled over at Gloria, who was sitting behind the barrier, her face beaming with pride.

Juliet was happy, too. She'd done the right thing by leaving Rochelle alone for a week to figure everything out for herself. Giving her the space she'd needed had paid off. What a difference it had made! Rochelle was now skating at her highest level. She'd started hesitantly, but almost immediately her nerves had settled, and she'd delivered a perfect performance.

Gloria cheered her on at the top of her voice.

"Well done, Rochelle. Amazing! You were fantastic!"

Rochelle grinned at her, uplifted by her words of encouragement. Skating was her life. She loved it so much. She was proud of herself.

It had been a tough week, but today was a good day. Her spirit had been tested, but not broken. She glanced over at Vanessa whose frustration was evident as she argued with her coach.

Vanessa had watched Rochelle's performance, and it had made her feel nauseous. Resentment and bitterness crept through her veins. She was fighting a constant internal battle. She couldn't control her envy of her old friend and, even though she didn't like herself for it, she was beginning to hate her!

Her eyes began to sting with unshed tears. She blinked them back before they ruined her mascara. There was a sadness dwelling within her. But, over the past week, she had taken great pleasure in the fact that Rochelle hadn't been attending her training sessions. In sharp contrast, she'd been practising hard all week. Surely, it must be giving her a considerable advantage.

Afterwards, Gloria drove Rochelle home.

"It's a shame about what's happened to my friendship with Vanessa. In point of fact, I don't even consider her as a friend anymore.

Over the last week, it's dawned on me that I might have been seeing her through rose-tinted glasses. I'm now having to face reality and put it all into perspective."

"I know, Rochelle. You need to realise that she's jealous of you. The problem for her is that you outshine her."

"I think it may have been her who's spread rumours about Lloyd and me … telling lies to the press. She doesn't seem to care about me anymore. The fun went out of our friendship a while ago. She always seems to be in a bad mood now. Did you see her arguing with her coach?"

"I did, yes. I'm glad you're seeing things with more clarity now, Rochelle. It appears that you can't trust her."

"Yeah! I've seen a few red flags lately. I need to be careful around her."

The build-up to the Winter Olympics commenced in earnest, and Rochelle was looking towards the event with optimism. She was putting in a lot of effort, taking chances with her programme, and her new-found self-confidence was leading her to believe it would all pay off.

Her ability to focus on her skating grew stronger, putting the troubled part of her mind to sleep. She'd bounced back through adversity.

Juliet's energy was a source of great inspiration, which lifted Rochelle to a higher plane. She motivated her with positive words, and whenever Rochelle saw Vanessa, she gave her a little wave, but then put her straight out of her mind.

In pushing herself to achieve her best, she took lots of falls on the ice, but each time it happened she tried hard to get it right the next time, facing each of the manoeuvres with even more determination. Her happiness soared as she visualised herself standing on the podium with a gold medal around her neck, and despite her differences with Vanessa, she still visualised her standing next to her wearing the silver medal, both of them smiling proudly at one another.

After another hard day of training, Rochelle dived thankfully onto her large, comfy bed, exhausted both mentally and physically. As she did so, she noticed a handwritten note on her pillow. It read:

'We love you, Rochelle. The day you entered our lives, our family was complete. We have watched you grow into an amazing young lady, and you fill our hearts with special pride and incredible joy.

Thank you for being such a lovely daughter.

Goodnight. Sleep tight.

Mum and Dad xxx'

She held the note to her heart and fell into a deep, contented sleep.

CHAPTER 21

On the final run-up to the Olympics, training was taking place in Grenoble.

They'd made it! They were both here as part of the British team … both Rochelle and Vanessa.

Their relationship had deteriorated even further. Vanessa had become more jealous and spiteful, and had gone as far as to label Rochelle as both a liar and a thief. The hurt all this had caused Rochelle she hid well from other people, as her tears spilled in silence into her pillow at night.

She was so disappointed. These moments should have been theirs to share … to enjoy … their reward for all the hard work and commitment they had endured over the years. Rochelle was determined it wouldn't spoil her time here, but she couldn't celebrate in the way she would have liked to. This should have been the most exciting time of their lives.

Rochelle observed Vanessa's attitude around the male Olympians. It made her sick to watch. She was making herself look like a flirty tart, wearing bright red lipstick, plastering her face in way-too-much makeup, and when not on the rink, dressing as though she was a hot, femme fatale. She was going too far, making a fool of herself in public. It was painful for Rochelle to witness.

After dinner, back in the privacy of her room, Rochelle stared out of the window at the beauty of the dense, snow-covered forest surrounding the hotel. She decided to throw on her bikini and towelling bathrobe, and head to the spa. She would swim a few lengths and then make use of the sauna and the Jacuzzi. It would be a relaxing end to a hard day of training.

Lying back with her eyes closed, she sensed that someone had entered the Jacuzzi beside her. She didn't want to open her eyes, so she breathed the person in. A male fragrance, for sure … a scent blended with woody notes and green olives. It smelt refreshing. Out of curiosity, she opened her eyes.

She didn't know why, but she suddenly felt nervous. Something about him and his close proximity in the large oval Jacuzzi turned her into a bumbling wreck. She glanced at his charming face. He was attractive by most people's standards. She found herself staring at him, her eyes transfixed. He stared straight back at her. A form of silent communication seemed to be taking place. He was the first male she had looked at in this way since Lloyd's death. The dark-haired, clean-shaven, young man smiled at her, and butterflies fluttered in the pit of her stomach.

"How are you? It's Rochelle isn't it? … the figure skater from Britain?"

"Yes, that's me. I'm fine, thanks. How do you know who I am?"

"I'm a figure skater, too, I'm Christoph! … Christoph Muller, and I'm Austrian."

There was a slight accent, but his English was perfect.

He laughed.

"I'm offended that you don't know who I am. I've seen you skate before. I like your perfume, by the way. You smell good."

She laughed. It was weird that the first thing she'd noticed about him, albeit with her eyes closed, had been his aftershave.

He raised both his arms above his head and leaned forwards stretching. Rochelle's eyes drifted to his strong, muscular shoulders. She averted them at once.

As she looked into his eyes, she questioned what type of soul lay beneath, and whether he had witnessed her heart skip a beat as their eyes locked.

"I'd like to take you to the beach when all the competitions and madness are over. Powdered, crystal sand between our toes, salt water in our mouths, and our noses filled with fragrant sea air! What could be better than that?"

Taken a little aback, she decided to play along with him.

"Ooh! Impressive. Where shall we go? I've always fancied the Caribbean myself. Dark Jamaican rum punch and mellow reggae music. We can snorkel under the white-fringed waves and hike the peaks."

His face brightened, and he laughed.

"I will make it one of the most memorable

delightful experiences of your life."

She knew her face was turning red; it was weird but also magical. She couldn't understand it, but she wanted him to kiss her … right there and then.

She was suddenly aware how dreadful her hair must look, wet and tied into a messy ponytail. She tried to adjust it a little. As she lowered her hand, he touched it with his, and held it beneath the bubbles. She allowed her hand to rest in his … it seemed the most natural thing in the world. It was as though she was back, dancing on the ice.

Her body was tingling with desire for him.

And then he did it … he leant towards her and kissed her, full on the lips.

Feeling bashful, she pulled away and asked, "Joking aside though, do you really want to travel after all this is over?"

"Yes! I'm sick of living my life in a bubble. I want to learn more about the world. This is the first time I've left England." She smiled at him. "Have you travelled much, outside of Austria?"

"Well, I've been to England. That's where I saw you skate. But otherwise not much … a few times to Germany and a few other places in Europe with my family, when I was younger."

"Christoph! I like your name. I've never met a Christoph before." She bit her lip in a flirtatious manner. "Anyway, I've got to go. I've a big schedule tomorrow. An early night is much needed."

Climbing out of the sunken Jacuzzi, she grabbed her fluffy, brown towel and robe from the side of the pool. She turned back towards him, gave him a shy smile, and then walked towards the changing rooms.

Back in her bed, she fell asleep dreaming about Christoph, the kiss and the sun-drenched, white sand beaches of the Caribbean.

The following morning at breakfast, Rochelle scanned the room, hoping to catch a glimpse of Christoph. Instead, she caught the eye of Vanessa.

She decided to approach her.

"Morning, Vanessa! Can we put everything behind us and be friends again?"

"No way, Rochelle. Who wants to be friends

with a liar and a thief?"

Rochelle blinked and stared off into the distance, determined not to shed a tear. She had been prepared to forgive Vanessa for her spitefulness, but she knew now that this was no longer an option. She watched her old friend glide back to an empty table with her breakfast tray.

Rather than remain anywhere near Vanessa, she decided to skip breakfast and headed straight for the women's training rink. Christoph would be at the men's rink, so there was no chance of bumping into him.

Juliet was already on the ice, waiting at the allocated time, as Rochelle skated towards her. She beamed at the tall, athletic woman, who had touched her heart and troubled mind during the many sessions they had spent together since she was an impulsive, quick-tempered, young girl. Juliet had always believed in Rochelle, even throughout her more testing moments. She had always kept her hopes and dreams alive, however impossible and grandiose they seemed, motivating her, confronting her inevitable setbacks and challenging her to become more resilient. She had always been able to recognise, and had worked hard to address,

Rochelle's emotional needs, as well as nurture her ambitions as a skater.

The training session went well, and Juliet had only enthusiastic praise to offer.

"You're doing great, Rochelle. I'm proud of you. Perhaps you should take this afternoon off. You've worked so hard. Everything's going to plan and I don't want to risk your suffering an injury by overdoing your training."

"That's brilliant! Thank you so much for all you've done for me, Juliet. You've been the best coach I could ever have wished for."

She gave her a quick, tight hug.

As Rochelle left the rink, she shielded her eyes from the brightness of the gleaming sun bouncing off the snow. A whole afternoon and evening to herself! How was she going to fill this unexpected luxury?

Back at the hotel, hunger gripped her. She'd skipped breakfast due to Vanessa, so she decided to get some lunch before going to her room to shower and change her clothes.

She was sitting in a quiet corner of the restaurant when she saw him.

Christoph!

Straight away, she noticed how chic he looked, dressed in a blue suit with a paler blue shirt and a brown tie. She could see he hadn't been training today. She wished she'd changed her own clothes before lunch now, and was wearing something smarter than a tracksuit and trainers.

Memories of Lloyd and a sense of guilt overwhelmed her. How could she be interested this way in someone else? She remembered how sweet and kind Lloyd had been towards her. She still missed him a great deal.

Out of the blue, she heard Lloyd's voice whispering in her ear.

"I'm all right, Rochelle. It's okay for you to look for love again."

She put her hand to her mouth and gasped. Her heart was thumping so fast. She blinked away the tears as a flashback of her parents' accident rushed through her mind.

Christoph's clear blue eyes widened as he raised his hand in an affectionate wave.

"Hi! You're not training today, then?"

"I was this morning, but my coach has given me the afternoon off."

She smiled, unaware of how pretty she looked, as her smile extended to her eyes and deep down into her soul.

She was overcome with a sudden, burning desire for him. What was happening to her? She didn't need this distraction from her skating … or did she? Part of her wanted to run … to bolt as far away as possible from him. The other part wished she was laying in his bed, wrapped in his sleek, muscular arms.

Christoph took the seat opposite her.

"You're probably aware of the rumours going around about you, Rochelle, both in the newspapers and in the Olympic village. *Are* you adopted? *Did* your parents die? *Were* you left orphaned?"

Although his questions were direct and personal, coming from him, they hadn't made her squirm. She answered him truthfully while Christoph listened caringly to her every word.

When she'd finished speaking, he asked, "Would you like to spend the rest of the day with me? I've no commitments for the rest of the afternoon, nor evening either,"

The tension lifted from her. Even though she'd told him everything, he still wanted to spend the afternoon with her – and perhaps the evening, as well.

"I'd love to!" she whispered.

She smiled at him, and her eyes sparkled.

At that moment Rochelle glanced across the elegant dining room and noticed Vanessa approaching their table. Her smile faded.

She was dressed like a tart again: tight, torn, black jeans with killer-heeled, thigh-high, black boots, a red vest top, which was too tight and showed more of her bust than was necessary, and she had large, gold-coloured, hooped earrings dangling from her rather long, earlobes. Her face was stern, and she looked as though she had plenty of attitude and red-faced anger to throw in Rochelle's direction. Without waiting to be asked, she pulled over a chair from an adjacent table and sat down beside them.

In a loud, grating voice she said, "This your brand-new, perfect boyfriend then? Over Lloyd are we then?"

Irritated, Rochelle rolled her eyes upwards. How could Vanessa have the audacity to speak to her in that way?

Her response shocked them all … even herself.

"Fuck you, Vanessa! As a matter of fact, I'm not interested in anything you've got to say to me! And anyway, no one asked you to join us."

CHAPTER 22

Christoph's deep tone of voice saved Rochelle from the situation with Vanessa.

"I don't know what's happening here, but Rochelle and I were about to go out for lunch."

He took hold of Rochelle's arm and guided her away from Vanessa to a place of safety in the hotel lobby.

Rochelle's breathing was short and quick.

"If you meant what you just said, I need to go to my room to shower and change. I can't go out for lunch dressed like this."

"Of course, I meant it. Hurry up, I'll wait for you here."

And so it was, an hour later, that Rochelle was walking arm in arm with Christoph along the streets of Grenoble, heading for a restaurant he said he thought she would love. Although the weather was freezing, her heart was warm and she was secure and safe, knowing he had removed her from a bad situation without demanding to know the reason for her outburst.

They wandered through the streets of the Old Town admiring the architecture, which seemed untouched by time, until they found the colourful, timber structure of the bistro they had been looking for.

As they took their seats at the rustic table, Rochelle removed her red scarf from her neck, the waiter having already taken her thick navy-blue coat to hang up for her.

"Are your parents coming out to watch the competitions, Rochelle?"

"Yes! They're due to arrive the day before they start. It's strange being here without them. Their names are Derek and Gloria, by the way. They've been good to me over the years. I wasn't an easy child. They've had to have a lot of patience with me.

"I haven't asked you much about yourself. What about your parents? Are they coming out?" Rochelle asked.

"No! My parents are no longer alive. Similar to your situation, they were killed in an accident – a cable car accident – two years ago."

"Oh! I'm sorry. I didn't know.

"Skating and the Olympics have kept me going … kept me focused. It was *their* dream as much as my own."

A brief hush overcame them, as they drifted off into their own thoughts.

Christoph broke the silence.

"When you choose your meal, make sure you leave enough room for the ice-cream. It's to die for here.

"By the way, I like your dress. It's a lovely colour."

She was pleased she'd changed into the turquoise dress. It was one of her favourites. Gloria had chosen it for her to bring away with her.

"Thank you. Gloria bought it for me. She told me to wear it for a special occasion."

Christoph smiled at her across the table.

"I want my life to become less stressful after the Olympics. Life's too short … as we both know."

"How come you don't have a girlfriend?"

"Haven't had the time … oh, and it may have something to do with not having met anyone I've found interesting."

"How about you? Lloyd! Who's he? You flew off the handle about him?"

"He was my boyfriend when we were young. He died in an accident, too. I guess you and I don't have much luck with people we care about.

"Anyway, let's change the subject. I love it here. Thanks for inviting me. It's so pretty with the window boxes full of red flowers … even though I don't know what they're called. And look at the snow-capped mountains! They're magnificent."

Christoph wiped a tear from his left eye with his serviette.

"I want to make you happy, Rochelle. I want to make us both happy."

They enjoyed each other's company for the entire duration of the hearty meal. They both felt relaxed, time seeming inconsequential as they pushed aside the pressures of the upcoming competitions.

"Vanessa was my closest friend, you know. I'm actually worried about her. She's changed so much. It's all so weird, how she's behaving. We've shared everything over the years. Her anger towards me seems to have reached boiling point, and I don't know what I've done to upset her. She's said some terrible things about me. I've tried my utmost to make things right between us, but I guess that today, I'd had enough."

"I'm sorry. It does seem strange that she's behaving like that."

He leant across the table and held her delicate hand tightly in his own.

"You're gorgeous, though. Maybe she's jealous that you outshine her in every way?"

She studied his face … those gorgeous blue eyes. He studied her back, taking in her natural beauty. It was as if their eyes took on a language of their own.

In her head, she stripped him naked. She raised her eyebrows. *"What?"* she thought and giggled a little in embarrassment as to where her thoughts had drifted. She lowered her head and looked at him almost childlike before she glanced away.

"I fancy the hell out of you, Rochelle," he

confessed.

"I find you attractive, too. I'm glad you fancy me."

"Shall we go back to the hotel … to my room?" he enquired seductively.

As they left the restaurant, she still hadn't replied to his question, but she turned to him and said, "How about a quick kiss now, whilst I make a decision?"

They leaned into each other and their lips locked in a long, lingering kiss. Their eyes closed as they drifted off for a brief moment into their own erotic fantasy world.

She tried to remain rational and not to allow her bodily desires to lead her into something she might regret. She needed to remain chilled … to rebalance her mind. Her head was in a battle with her body.

He kissed her again, igniting her passion once more. It was exquisite, magical, wonderful and bedazzling. It was all so exciting, the blood awakening her brain as he used his gentle tongue, and she ventured back with hers. Deep within her chest, and in every cell of her body, she felt a warm, blissful peace. Love had surfaced in her heart. Her instincts told her this was right. It was a beautiful dream. She knew that whatever happened from now on, she would remember this day forever.

"I can see you need a little more persuasion. My room has a hot tub on the balcony. We could order a bottle of champagne and some strawberries. Are you tempted?"

"I wanted to anyway, but you've definitely persuaded me now. I'll need to go to my room and grab my bikini first, though."

"You're joking! You need a bikini? Are you sure? We could skinny dip. Nobody can see us; it's private."

They walked at a sedate pace back to the exclusive hotel, holding hands in a hushed silence. On arrival, Rochelle rushed to her room to grab her bikini. She had decided to put it on underneath her long, towelling bath robe, as if she was going to the fancy, four-star spa.

Only, she wasn't going to the spa, she was going to Christoph's room … to spend time in a hot tub with the strong, handsome man she fancied like crazy.

On leaving her room, she took a look at herself in the wall-mounted mirror and said, "You can do this."

He opened the door to her discreet knock, but straight away she could see that something was wrong.

"I'm sorry, but I've had some terrible news. One of my best friends was killed in a luge practice run early this morning. He lost control of his sled. The news channels haven't broken the story yet, so please don't repeat it to anyone."

Rochelle inched back towards the corridor.

"I'm so sorry. Let's do this some other time."

Back in her room, she lay on her bed curled up in the foetus position, nursing her pain for the loss of all the people she'd loved in the past. She felt Christoph's pain now, too. She shouldn't have let herself get close to anyone again. It happened every time. More pain on top of pain.

She switched on the TV trying to distract herself, but nothing caught her attention as she flicked through the channels. Her thoughts drifted back to Christoph. What had she discovered about him so far? Well, she knew he was down-to-earth and sensible, no fly-by-night fool. And he must have been dedicated to his skating to have got this far.

He seemed loyal, too; she'd witnessed this by his reaction to his friend's death. She liked the fact that he had immediately changed his mind about spending time with her, and had given himself space to come to terms with the terrible accident. But, she still found him mysterious and longed to learn more about him.

She decided to Google him to find out what sort of chance he had of winning a medal. She knew with certainty he wasn't one of the favourites – she already knew who they were – but at the Olympics, it didn't mean a thing. A couple of bad falls or an injury and the outcome of the medals could all change.

She thought about his body – strong, powerful and athletic. His face seemed to be chiselled in stone, and he had a serious expression. He dressed in a European style – chic – not like the boys she knew back home. He was so sexy.

Shit! She couldn't lie here doing this to herself. She needed to shower and find something to do before she drove herself crazy. There was still most of the afternoon and all of the evening left, which she'd seen as a luxury until she'd heard the news about Christoph's friend.

She took a long, soothing shower and relaxed back on the bed while she listened to her meditation CD. The rhythmic percussion of waves on sand calmed her thoughts as she tried to decide what to do with the rest of her day. Tired and drained as she was from all of her recent heavy training, she drifted off to sleep in the soft afternoon sunlight that streamed in through her window.

A firm knock at her door woke her. Pulling on her favourite comfy jeans and t-shirt, she shouted, "Hang on, I'm coming. Give me a minute."

She opened the door and her face washed blank with confusion, as she found Christoph standing there, grinning from ear to ear.

"Aren't you going to invite me in?" he asked.

"Yes! But why are you grinning? She didn't return his smile, believing his behaviour a little strange for someone who'd received such bad news just a short time ago.

"Can you believe it!" he scoffed. "He's not dead! Somebody played a cruel trick on me. He wasn't even in an accident. He's one hundred percent fine."

Closing the door behind them she said, "I

don't understand. What do you mean somebody played a cruel prank on you? Who could be so mean?"

It took her a while, but Vanessa suddenly sprang to mind. But, would she stoop so low? Why not? She'd already branded Rochelle a liar and a thief.

"I'm sorry that someone could have been so cruel."

"And I'm sorry it ruined our wonderful day! But at least it's not true, which is obviously an immense relief."

Rochelle's eyes searched his face.

"It's horrible to think this way, but I've a bizarre belief that Vanessa's behind all this."

"Oh, my God! Would she be capable of doing something like this?"

She trembled as they sat next to each other on the bed. He placed his hand on hers.

"Let's not let it ruin the rest of the time we have today. We've wasted enough of it already. If it is her, we're only letting her achieve what she set out to do."

She gave him a wan smile.

"You don't want to know how much she's

already hurt me. She was my best friend for a long time. I trusted her."

"Let's forget about her. She's not worth it. Put a nice dress on, and we'll go out for a few drinks and dinner. I'll go and freshen up, and I'll knock your door in about an hour."

"Fabulous, but I can't drink too much, nor stay out too late, as I have training in the morning."

"Me, too. We won't overdo it."

As she looked through her modest wardrobe trying to decide what to wear, anger towards Vanessa began to grow deep within her. What else was she capable of doing?

Her impatient hands moved through her rather limited wardrobe. *A nice dress,* he'd said. But he'd already seen one of the few she owned. She had another special one, which again Gloria had chosen for her: a flattering, floral-print, silk-georgette little number. Rochelle had said it was far too expensive, but Gloria had insisted on treating her.

After taking longer over her make-up than she'd ever done before, she stood back and observed herself in the full-length mirror. It dawned on her how much she cared about how Christoph saw her. Was this love? She wasn't sure. How could you define the word love?

Eventually, she heard the long-anticipated knock on her bedroom door. As they walked arm in arm, through the hotel lobby, a young girl approached and asked for her autograph. Rochelle still hadn't got used to the fact that people recognised her, and it was always a particularly pleasant surprise when someone younger than herself asked for her autograph.

The young girl thanked her.

"You'll win the gold, Rochelle Erickson," she told her.

Christoph laughed.

"I wonder where all of *my* fans are hiding? Anyway, if my skating doesn't impress you, I'm hoping to do it in other ways. Tonight, you are my lady. I've booked a car to collect us. The whole night is on me. My treat!"

"Thank you. That's so kind of you. And, by the way, I think you should still go for the gold. The odds may be against you, but you've got as much chance of winning as anyone else," she said.

As they climbed into the rear of the flashy, German car, Rochelle wanted to sing aloud from the distant rooftops, such was her happiness at the beauty of her life at that moment. She intended to make the most of tonight, and enjoy it to its full. Driving westward, hand in hand, the purest white snow danced in the headlights like a scene from a Christmas card. The trees were adorned with glowing fairy lights and her heart buzzed with excitement.

Their first port of call was a circular, rooftop cocktail bar in a lavish hotel, where they sat outside under electric heaters, wrapped in cosy woollen blankets. Sparks flew around them and Rochelle wasn't sure whether it was the effect that Christoph was having on her, or the two cocktails she'd consumed. She decided it was in all likelihood a combination of the two. Everything was happening like a whirlwind.

Before she knew it, she found herself enveloped in the warmth of Christoph's arms as he embraced her, but something nagged in her subconscious that this was all too good to be true, and somehow her beautiful dream would soon be shattered. She studied his big, strong hands as he held tightly onto hers.

They leant back in their chairs to watch the spectacular sunset, and then moved closer together as twilight crept slowly across the sky. The ferocity of her feelings for Christoph astonished her. She felt that she was complete in his company. She was safe. It was all so natural. She looked into his eyes and beamed at him, knowing without question she had something to smile about.

"Thank you for tonight, Christoph. This is enchanting."

"It's not over yet; this is only the beginning. Anyway, I'm the lucky one! I can't believe that you wanted to spend it with me."

He grinned and winked at her.

They finished their fourth cocktail, and Rochelle was surprised to find their bearded driver and the luxurious car still waiting outside to take them to the restaurant that Christoph had booked for them.

"This must be costing you a fortune! I can't let you pay for all of this."

"Don't worry about it. I told you it was my treat."

After a steep climb up the southwest high road, which was swathed on either side by rows of tall, snow-covered trees, her spirit began to dance. They arrived at an expensive-looking, mountainside restaurant. The high-powered, noiseless car turned into the sweeping driveway, and the courteous driver opened the solid, metal door to allow her an unimpeded exit. She felt as though she was an international celebrity and she revelled in it.

As they entered the fine restaurant Christoph said, "It's an eighteenth-century, castle-like villa. Don't you just love it?'

It looked a little fancy to her, but she didn't want to say so.

"Yes, it's gorgeous," she agreed.

She took in her surroundings: dark wooden furniture, beige curtains and glistening chandeliers. The hostess guided them to their table.

As they took their seats, Christoph gave her a quick kiss. Once they had been provided with their menus and the hostess had moved away, Rochelle was surprised as Christoph's hand slid below the table and stroked her knee tenderly.

"Shall I choose us some wine?"

"I'm not sure. I'm already a bit tipsy."

"Oh, come on. Let's enjoy ourselves. Make the most of it. We've worked hard enough.

One night won't hurt."

Plain and simple, she was drunk. But to hell with it. He was right. One daring night wouldn't matter, would it?

The wine arrived, and they gave the waitress their orders. They decided to skip the starters and both ordered a grilled steak, declaring that they were too tipsy to eat much.

"I can't remember the last time I've drunk alcohol like this," she giggled, feeling happy and helpless.

A vivid camera flash lit their table.

"Did someone just take a photograph of us?" she said, looking around.

They finished their meal quickly.

"Let's get back to the hotel … back to privacy. I didn't know you were such a celebrity," he joked.

Back at the hotel, he walked Rochelle back to her room.

"I'd love to spend the night with you, but I know we've both had a lot to drink. I wouldn't want to put any pressure on you."

"I'd love to as well, Christoph, but you're right. I'm still a virgin, and I don't want to do anything I'll regret in the morning. We both have early starts, so let's do the sensible thing and kiss goodnight here."

"You are beautiful."

Like a spring flower opening, she smiled back at him and moved into his strong and agile arms, draping her own around his neck. Her parted lips fitted perfectly against his and, unable to resist, they kissed with a violent passion. She stepped back.

"Too much wine," she slurred, as the corridor spun around her.

She clicked open her hotel room door.

"Goodnight Christoph. Thank you. I've had so much fun."

The following morning, sporting dark shadows under her eyes and being half an hour late for her intensive training session, Rochelle could see straight away that Juliet was unimpressed.

"I'm sorry I'm late. I was sick," she said, ashen faced.

Juliet flung the folded newspaper in Rochelle's anguished face. There was a photo of her and Christoph pasted all over the front page with the headline, *'Dedicated Rochelle! But Dedicated to what?'*

"What's all this about? Were you drinking? Vanessa's right on your tail, you know. You won't stand out like this. You'll be one or two steps behind her. You're making yourself look cheap and unreliable. This isn't going to give you a competitive edge. You're smarter than this. Look at the headline, Rochelle. They're questioning your dedication."

Rochelle was shocked. She couldn't remember Juliet ever being so angry with her. On the verge of bursting into tears, she tried to explain herself. Her legs were trembling and her fingers were shaking.

"It wasn't how it looks, Juliet. We had dinner together, and a couple of drinks."

"You don't need this type of distraction. Not now … not when you're so close to taking the gold medal. To tell you the truth, Rochelle, you stink of alcohol. How much did you drink?"

"I'm sorry. I did drink too much. I got carried away. I like him a lot and I was having fun. He spoiled me rotten. I didn't do anything stupid though. I slept in my own bed, on my own."

"Well, thank goodness for that. Are you fit to skate this morning, or not?"

"Yeah! I'll be fine … more or less. I'm sorry again."

She slid into the routine of her programme, and focused on the first and trickiest jump of the day. At the break, it was embarrassing as they sat in a sullen, ominous silence, Rochelle knowing without Juliet having to point it out to her that she hadn't skated well. She was ashamed. Why had she drunk so much?

She spotted Vanessa dispensing a drink from the vending machine. It didn't look as though her day was going much better than her own, as she'd obviously been crying and her face was full of pain.

An announcement over the tannoy took Rochelle by surprise. Shock registered on her face.

"Would Rochelle Erickson, please report to reception."

Rochelle looked at Juliet. A little wary and alarmed, they both rushed to the reception area. A florist greeted them with a huge bouquet of beautiful, vibrant flowers. The envelope was addressed to Rochelle.

Shaking and nervous – and the tiniest bit embarrassed – she froze as she read the card aloud.

'To Rochelle,

A heartfelt thank you for a very special night, one I shall never forget.

Now, focus on winning the gold medal, and when it's around your neck, I'd like to take you out in style, if you'll allow me.

With love,

Christoph'

Rochelle beamed at Juliet,

"C'mon! Stop worrying. Let's go practise and get that gold!"

CHAPTER 23

Gloria and Derek arrived in Grenoble the day before the opening ceremony. It was a rest day for Rochelle and her happiness overflowed when she greeted them in the hotel lobby, thrilled that they were there to support her and cheer her on. She had missed them tremendously, having never spent so much time away from them since she had first moved in. She revelled in their unconditional love and attention, and their presence gave her more confidence and security.

Hugging Rochelle tightly, Gloria said, "This is all so exciting, isn't it! If truth be told, I can't believe we're here. What a beautiful hotel. Shall we have lunch here?"

As they tucked into their lunches, Rochelle studied Derek, who had been quiet since they'd arrived. She noticed the crow's feet etched deeply into the corners of his eyes. He looked tired. Perhaps the journey had worn him out … but she couldn't help noticing that he was beginning to show his age.

He looked across at Rochelle.

"I'm so proud of you, you know: the qualities that have shone through you to get you here, your grit and resilience against all the odds that have been thrown at you. It's only through your own vision and determination that you've come this far."

Rochelle beamed as this unfamiliar praise from Derek sunk in.

"Thank you, Dad, but I couldn't have done any of this without the moral and material support that you and Mum have given me. You gave me a happy family life, when I no longer had one. You helped me to have a healthy mindset, despite everything I've experienced, and you challenged me to be a better person."

She grinned at both of them.

"Well, I'm going to order myself an Irish whiskey to celebrate being here," Derek said, "and I shall raise a glass to you, Rochelle, for making us such proud, lucky and fortunate parents. The day you entered our lives was the best day ever. We've never regretted it once, not even on your lowest of dark days."

"How's Vanessa coping with her parents' divorce? Are they coming out to support her?" Gloria asked.

"Whoa! Back up! What did you say? When did that happen? We haven't had a proper conversation in ages. I had no idea. That explains why she's been acting so strangely, and why she's been so mean to me."

"Oh! Sorry, pet! Didn't you know? I wasn't aware that things had become so bad between you."

"I can't believe they're getting divorced. They seemed so happy together. Perfect parents, in fact. I need to go and find Vanessa, and see if she'll talk to me now that I know what's going on. Do you mind if I go now? I need to talk to her before the competitions begin. Poor Vanessa!"

Rochelle found Room 103 and banged her fist on the door.

"Hang on! I'm coming. Stop banging as if you're trying to wake the dead," Vanessa shouted.

She looked startled to discover that it was

Rochelle who'd been doing the banging, but with the door wide open, she was unable to stop Rochelle from entering her room and plonking herself on the bed, just as if they were still best friends.

"I'm so sorry! Why didn't you tell me? I've only just found out about your parents.

"What's happened to us? Where did it all go wrong? I need to know. We've shared so much, and now you can't even tell me about your parents' divorce. I had to find out from Gloria. All the fun we've shared in the past, all thrown away! Over what, Vanessa?"

"I'm just full of anger. Don't waste your time on me. There's no point."

"Angry about what? Your parents? Or something I did?"

"I say and do things I don't mean to."

"Why are you so hostile?"

"Don't you see? You're my rival! My bitter enemy! You have it all."

"How on earth did you come to that conclusion, Vanessa? It's crazy."

"I can't tell you."

"Tell me what?"

"I can't tell you!"

" Tell me! I want to forgive you, so that we can be friends again."

"What if my life's not all it's cracked up to be?"

"You've lost me, Vanessa. I don't understand what you're trying to say."

"I'm useless! My life is worthless."

"Don't be so stupid! What are you talking about? You're about to compete for the gold medal at the Olympics. It's everything you've worked so hard for ... *we've* worked so hard for, in fact."

"But what is it that we've we worked for? In terms of skill, yes, I find it easy now, but what if I don't *feel* it anymore?"

"Oh, Vanessa! You can't come this far, and then feel like this now. That's too sad."

"But it's just skating to me now. There's no longer any thrill."

"How can you say that? It's been our passion for as long as I can remember."

"That's not true for me. It's always been *your* passion. I've just been dragged along by you."

Nausea clawed at Rochelle's throat, and she

felt as though she was about to vomit.

"It's not real for me now, Rochelle. When I skate, it's like I'm damn well watching myself from above."

Uncertain of how to respond, Rochelle remained silent, holding firmly onto Vanessa's hand.

"At some point, skating took over our lives. Don't you see it? We're living in a false reality," Vanessa said.

"But why alienate me? What did I do to deserve it?"

"I don't know."

"Well, you should know. You've done and said some terrible things."

"Well, I'm tired as hell of this conversation. Can you go now?"

"No! I'm not giving up on you, Vanessa."

"For fuck's sake, give up on me! I'm not worth it. You don't even know the half of it."

"We used to tell each other everything. Don't you remember? We had no secrets from one another."

"Well, I guess some secrets are too big to share."

"Nothing can be so big to have risked losing our friendship. I don't understand what it is you can't tell me."

"Have you any idea what it's like to be in love with your best friend?"

"I don't understand! What do you mean?"

"I invested so much time in you, Rochelle, that I fell in love with you."

"Well, I love you, too. I still do, even after all you've done."

"I don't mean the *friendship* type of love … I mean I fancy you. I want to be with you … the *other* type of love."

"Oh, God! I didn't know. Is this what this is all about? Why didn't you tell me before? We can deal with this. It doesn't mean we can't be friends, does it? I mean, I don't have those sort of feelings about you, but we don't have to hate one another, do we?"

"I've got my life in a mess over this. There's more …"

"More! How can there be more? What have you done?"

"I appreciate that you still care, Rochelle, especially after all I've done to you … but I can't talk about the rest of it.

"Can you give me some space now, please? I'm so tired. You've got half of the answer you came for. I love you! That's all there is to it! And I'm sorry for the horrible things I've done."

Rochelle got up and walked towards the door.

"I'm sorry you've been so miserable, Vanessa, and you didn't trust me enough to tell me about all this. But, now it's out in the open, can we at least be civil with one another? And if you want to talk about the other stuff at any time, I'm in Room 304."

Back at the restaurant with Gloria and Derek, Rochelle decided not to tell them about the conversation she'd just had with Vanessa. In reality, she hadn't sorted it all out in her own head yet … and anyway, how do you tell your parents that your best friend has just told you that she's in love with you?

As they chatted about everyday stuff, Rochelle's eyes flitted around the room, looking to see if Christoph was around. He wasn't … but she became aware of the conversation on the table next to them. She overheard Vanessa's name being mentioned, so she strained her ears to try and glean what was being said.

"Well, it's not even as though she's from a poor background! I've heard she's had quite a privileged upbringing," one woman said.

The other woman responded, "She's awful. She wears terrible clothes … and have you seen how short her hair is now she's had it cut? She looks like a lesbian."

It seemed the Olympic village was turning out to be just as ruthless as Juliet had warned her it would be. There were lots of rumours flying around. Unable to listen to any more of their conversation without butting in and defending her friend, Rochelle made her excuses to her parents and headed for the bathroom. She stared at her reflection in the mirror, questioning why people would be so vicious. She decided that she needed to clear her head of both Christoph and Vanessa until the competitions were over, otherwise she would tear herself to shreds.

Turning around she tripped over a mop and bucket. Cursing, she told herself to focus on the gold medal. She couldn't allow her emotions to run amok now. This wasn't the time to have a meltdown.

She found her way back to the security of Gloria and Derek, and was relieved to see that the women on the next table were paying their bill and leaving.

"We've missed you so much, Rochelle," Gloria told her. "It seems ages since you came out here to train."

"Are you skating well?" Derek asked.

"I'm making the most of it. I want to enjoy the whole experience."

"Have you decided what you'd like to do after all this is over?" Gloria asked.

"Yes, I want to travel … to see some more of the world."

Hours later, Rochelle tucked herself into bed, having spent a pleasant evening with Gloria and Derek. There had been no sign of Christoph, which hadn't been a bad thing as she wasn't quite ready to explain about him to her parents yet. After all, it wasn't as though they were in a permanent relationship.

She had managed to put Vanessa out of her mind for the time being, although she was very worried about her, and also about what the other secret may be. She read for a little, before placing her book on the bedside table. As she drifted off to sleep, her thoughts were of the opening ceremony, which was to take place the following day.

Rochelle's alarm woke her at 7am. She intended to have a relaxed morning, with no distractions, before meeting with the rest of the team to prepare to parade into the Olympic stadium in the afternoon.

Ready way ahead, and with copious free time on her hands, she waited anxiously, pacing around her hotel room at the proverbial snail's pace, trying to while away the time. Her mind drifted to Christoph, and wondered whether she would see him later at the magical opening ceremony.

A brisk knock at her door made her jump. Upon opening it, she was surprised to find Christoph standing there.

"You okay?"

She smiled as she spoke.

"Yeah! Have you had breakfast yet?"

"No! I wasn't hungry. I know I should eat something, but I'm way too excited."

"Well, let me in and we'll order room

service. You need to eat. We can't have you passing out during the parade."

A warm, fuzzy glow overcame her as she closed the door behind him and watched as he picked up the room service menu.

"So … what would Mademoiselle like to order? Or shall I order for both of us?"

Breakfast ordered, Christoph turned to Rochelle.

"What are your costumes like for the competitions? Can I see them? Or do you want to keep them a secret?"

"A guarded secret, of course! I don't even have them here. My coach, Juliet, has locked them away somewhere safe. She says that my costumes are almost as important as my performance. But I, personally, think that's a load of rubbish! "

Their breakfast arrived, and they ate it in silence, Rochelle contemplating the next few nerve-wracking days ahead.

CHAPTER 24

Rochelle stood waiting in line, along with the rest of the Great Britain team, to walk through the tunnel as part of the opening ceremony of the Winter Olympics. She kept glancing over at Vanessa, who was not looking her normal self and kept coughing. She looked pale and was wearing no make-up.

Although she knew she wasn't responsible for Vanessa, she still wanted to help her. They had shared the same dream for a very long time, and now the time was here, it wasn't turning out to be the glittering occasion they had believed it was going to be. Rochelle could hardly recognise her once beautiful friend with her bleached-blonde, cropped hairstyle. They'd come so far, and now it was all so different between them.

Rochelle thought back to the time when

they'd both put in huge efforts to get to this stage, remembering all the fun they'd shared playing around at the rink when they'd not been training. Feeling a little nostalgic, she wished she could turn back time. But then she checked herself. This was *her* time ... *her* dream! She couldn't allow Vanessa to destroy it all. She imagined herself skating in front of the crowds and the television cameras.

She smiled over at Vanessa, but experienced a sharp ache in her heart as Vanessa blanked her. They walked through the tunnel and out into the stadium: the two of them, side by side, the flag bearer ahead of them waving the fluttering silk flag of Great Britain.

There was loud cheering and applauding from the crowds. Rochelle beamed. She was so proud of herself ... to be here representing her country. She wanted to relish this moment forever. The gold medal was hers for the taking.

But, at the same time, it was ludicrous, because, despite all the glamour of the occasion, Rochelle couldn't help herself from glancing over at Vanessa and remembering how much she had loved having her as a friend. She could tell that Vanessa wasn't enjoying this at all. It had been their joint goal, the pinnacle of all they had worked for, but now it would always be tinged with an edge of sadness.

She couldn't help but wonder what the other part of the secret was … the secret Vanessa had been unable to trust her with?

Vanessa moved closer to her and whispered, "Were we ever on the same side?"

Rochelle's face darkened.

"Of course, we were. We were best friends, remember. We still can be."

As she glanced over at Vanessa again, she was alarmed to see that her skin had taken on a glossy shine, and she was trembling.

She mouthed, "Are you okay?"

Shaking her head to indicate that she wasn't, she mouthed back, "I've taken some drugs."

Linking arms to steady Vanessa, Rochelle whispered, "You stupid sod! What the hell have you taken?"

"I'm sorry."

Looking around, embarrassed and annoyed, Rochelle whispered, "You'll have to pretend you're okay. Keep smiling. Don't forget the television cameras are on us, and could zoom in on our faces at any point."

"Thank you for being so kind."

"Focus! Concentrate on your walking and pull your shoulders back. We'll be out in the arena for about 20 minutes. You have to get through this."

The magical ceremony had turned into an excruciating nightmare. There weren't many options open to Rochelle other than to prevent Vanessa from either collapsing or making an even worse spectacle of herself. It was a terrible situation, and she hoped the damned cameras would be occupied elsewhere, and wouldn't turn their focus on them.

The 20 further distressing minutes seemed to last a lifetime, and it was a great relief when they headed back into the long, airless tunnel, away from the prying eyes of the excited crowds and the long-range cameras.

Anger boiled deep inside Rochelle, as Vanessa now became a whole different version of herself … all sunshine and mischievous smiles … as though none of the previous stuff had happened. Didn't she have the faintest idea of the anguish she had inflicted on Rochelle? Did she have any idea at all what could have happened in the arena, and what the disastrous consequences could have been for them both? … Never mind the fact that she'd completely ruined Rochelle's personal enjoyment of the special ceremony. It was as if Vanessa had blocked out the whole experience and didn't care about it. Rochelle wanted to slap the stupid smile off Vanessa's pathetic face.

Back in Vanessa's hotel room, where Rochelle had all but dragged her back to, Vanessa was now denying that she had taken any drugs and that she'd been fine all of the time. She told Rochelle that she had overreacted to the situation.

"I'm not keeping anything under wraps, Rochelle. I promise."

"I saw you! I saw the effect the drugs had on you!"

"Don't tell anyone, will you?"

"Have you been taking drugs often?"

How dare you insult me? You have no right."

"I could report you and have you tested."

"You really don't care about me, do you,

Rochelle? Is this the only way you can beat me to the gold medal?"

Rochelle remained silent, unable to respond.

"The way you carry on Rochelle, it's as if skating is a matter of life and death."

"For Christ's sake, how dare you! Do you know what you've put me through this afternoon?"

"Fuck you!"

"How can you be so flippant about taking drugs?"

"Okay! So I've been doing a bit of MDMA. I'm not addicted or anything."

"It's a Class A drug, Vanessa! We learned all about it at school."

"It gives me more energy."

"So, what about today? You looked awful. You were sweating, and you could barely co-ordinate your legs."

"I don't take much. Okay maybe I did overdo it today."

"Do you even know the importance of what you did?"

Pouting her lips, Vanessa smirked.

To Rochelle, that was like waving a bright red rag at an already enraged bull.

"What are you smirking about?"

All at once, the juvenile smile changed to a surge of noiseless tears. Vanessa dabbed at them with a tissue.

"I'm not sure I can help you," Rochelle said, stepping forward to take Vanessa's hand.

She snatched it away.

"Can I trust you?"

"Do you realise you're dicing with death? You could overdose at any time. It's like playing Russian roulette! Where have you been getting it from, anyway?"

"I know the risks."

"You don't, else you wouldn't do it, especially in your position. What if your drugs test comes back positive and you get disqualified? It would be all over the papers and you'd get arrested. They'd come down on you like a ton of bricks. They'd do it to set an example."

"It's hard to trace. It won't show up in my tests."

"And what about the danger to your health?

Aren't you at all bothered?"

"I only take a small amount."

"I've already lost enough people in my life: my parents and Lloyd. I don't want to lose you as well. In actual fact, I'm dumbfounded that you're okay with all this."

Vanessa shed more tears.

"The pressure of the whole world watching me skate is too much for me."

"It *is* overwhelming, to be honest."

"I've been going mad."

"I guess the pressure has got to you. Have you spoken with your coach about it?"

"Yes! All she ever says is that I'm lazy, and I'm putting on too much weight."

Rochelle narrowed her eyes.

"If she does that, then she's totally unprofessional. Juliet would never speak to me in those terms."

"I told her I wasn't sure I even wanted to take part in the Olympics."

"C'mon, Vanessa! We can still do this. It's our dream, remember! … One of us with the gold medal, and the other with the silver. It doesn't matter which way around it is."

"I will do it, Rochelle! I'll do it for you!"

"That's great. Anyway, I've got to go. I'm meeting Gloria and Derek for dinner," she lied.

Back in her own room, Rochelle reflected on the strange day she'd had. She'd lied to Vanessa about meeting Gloria and Derek in order to get away. She needed time to get her head straight, and to 'ground' herself. The short-program competition was scheduled for the following day. She had to focus, and drive all of Vanessa's problems out of her own mind. She was disgusted by the fact that Vanessa had been taking drugs, although it did explain some of her recent odd behaviour.

At least, she now knew what her other secret was!

She pushed the food around on the blue plate her room service meal had been delivered on. Her appetite had been depleted by the infuriating events of the day.

Her mobile rang. It was Gloria and Derek calling to wish her the best of luck for the following day.

After taking a long relaxing bath, pungent

with the fragrance of jasmine, she washed her hair, brushed her teeth and put on her pyjamas.

Her emotions towards Vanessa were mixed. On the one hand, she was angry, especially as she had ruined the opening ceremony for her. But on the other hand she was sorry for her … she had messed up so much.

Her phone rang again, and she was overjoyed to hear Christoph's voice on the line. He wished her success for tomorrow. She wished him the same, and a warm glow flowed through her when he said he couldn't wait to see her again after the competitions were all over.

She climbed into the big, comfortable bed, exhausted and pleased to be alone.

Just then, her phone pinged. It was a message from Vanessa. She opened it. It read:

'I love you, Rochelle. I'm sorry. I'll make it all okay tomorrow, I promise. I'll be skating for you.'

Her stomach somersaulted, but she messaged back.

'It's okay! I know you didn't mean any of this. We can be friends again.

Let's go get those medals.'

Chewing on her lip, Rochelle fell asleep.

CHAPTER 25

Juliet moved Rochelle's hand away from her mouth, where she had been gnawing at her nails.

"What's the matter? You don't bite your nails as a rule. Let's get you on the rink for some warm ups before they announce the order of competitors."

Once she was on the ice, Rochelle's muscles relaxed.

Standing on the edge of the rink, she informed Juliet, "I didn't sleep well last night. I felt nauseous for most of it."

"It's understandable. It's an adrenaline rush, given what you're due to face today."

"I'm so nervous."

"It's to be expected. Have a little skate

around, and then we'll go to my room and do some meditation."

"It'll be tough skating in front of so many people."

" You're liked, Rochelle. The crowd will be behind you."

"I'm concerned about Vanessa. Have you seen her this morning?"

"Have you two made up, then?"

"Sort of, but she's finding the Olympics so stressful."

"You're different from her, Rochelle. Her behaviour out here hasn't been great, and I'm afraid it hasn't gone unnoticed. You're better off severing your ties with her."

Rochelle skated off to complete her warm up, alarmed by the harsh picture Juliet had just painted of Vanessa – even though she knew her grim words were true.

'Well, screw it!' she thought.

She still cared about her, didn't she! She was still her friend ... despite everything she'd done. She needed to save Vanessa from herself. She was the closest thing she'd ever have to a sister.

"Ready for some meditation now?" Juliet shouted across the ice.

"You bet! Let's go for it."

"By the way, Vanessa's here. She's on her mobile over by the café."

"Good! That's music to my ears. I'm relieved she's here."

Rochelle lay on the bed in Juliet's training room, her eyes closed, listening to the meditation tape explaining about emotional balance. The technique worked well for her, as the positive words registered in her mind.

After the meditation had come to an end, Juliet suggested it was time to find out the skating order for the first competition.

"There are thirty competitors. You will be placed into three groups – ten skaters in each. There will be a short interval between each group for them to clean the ice," she said.

"Well, it's now or never," Rochelle said. "I need the loo first, though."

Washing her hands, she caught sight of Vanessa standing behind her in the mirror.

Vanessa spoke first.

"I saw you come in here. I've been looking

for you all morning. They're about to announce the skating order. Can I stand with you? I *so* wanna be in the same group as you."

Smiling, Rochelle said, "C'mon then! Let's go and find out."

Surrounded by skaters from all the other countries, they waited, arms linked, for their names to be read out. The woman announcer started to read the names from her list. Rochelle hopped from one foot to another with excitement, her knees shaking.

The woman named Vanessa as being in sixth position in the first group of ten. She looked across at Rochelle and crossed her fingers.

"Four places left. Please be in this group. I need you."

Placing an affectionate arm around Vanessa's narrow waist, Rochelle gave her a sympathetic squeeze.

Rochelle's mouth was dry with anticipation, every nerve in her body and brain electrified as she listened for her name to be read out.

Then it came.

"Number nine, Rochelle Erickson."

Vanessa let out a little giggle.

"Yes! Yes! Yes!"

"So we get to skate in the first ten. Let's show them, I know we can do it. Our individual performances have to be brilliant, better than any of the others."

"What colour are you wearing? I'm in blue," Vanessa said.

The short program competition started at two o'clock. The stadium was full to capacity as the first skater took to the ice. Rochelle's palms were sweaty as she watched the girl skate to the centre of the rink to take up her starting position. She could sense the girl's fear from the side of the rink, skating first in front of such a large audience. She noticed the girl was slouching a little, and reminded herself to keep her back straight when it was her turn to skate out into the centre.

Her real parents' faces popped into her mind. They would have been so proud of her today … she knew it in her heart. *Practice makes perfect!',* the words repeated by Juliet so often during their training, rung in her ears. She hoped Vanessa would rise to the occasion, but she knew she often skated stronger in practice than in front of a crowd.

One or two falls, and it could all be lost.

She visualised her program, rehearsing the routine in her mind. To score the big points, she needed to execute the major jumps particularly well. Using the positive thinking techniques that Juliet had taught her, she imagined the crowd applauding her as she curtsied to the judges and skated off the ice, knowing she had achieved the best she was capable of. She was Rochelle, the orphan kid no one had loved until Derek and Gloria had rescued her. Well, here was her chance to make the whole world love her.

Her focus returned to the girl on the ice. Her connection with the audience was immediate; she had them in the palm of her hand. Her delivery of the set program was good. This was it: the start of the real thing. The girl skated off the ice to massive applause. She'd skated well. Rochelle performed some stretching exercises whilst they waited for the next skater. Vanessa was at the other side of the rink with her coach. Rochelle was relieved; she didn't need any distractions at this particular moment.

As the second skater took to the ice, Rochelle felt the adrenaline begin to surge through her body again. The slim, 25-year-old was one of the first-rate Canadian skaters, and she was in with a good chance of winning a medal. Her balanced and professional performance was stunning and dynamic. Her striking red costume was exquisite and drew attention to her perfect figure. She skated both skilfully and gracefully, with an inexhaustible vitality, and the joy the Canadian experienced through her skating was plain to see. There was a radiant energy about her, which the first skater had lacked.

When it was Vanessa's turn to skate, Rochelle watched with apprehension as she took centre stage on the ice. Her choice of music was a wise one: *'Your Love Keeps Lifting Me Higher'* by Jackie Wilson. She opened her program with real passion and straight away performed the classic spiral spin, which no one else, including Rochelle, could pull off in the same surprising and astonishing manner as she did. Her whole agile body seemed to engage with the spin. She was as graceful as a swan, with her narrow hips, powerful shoulders, and long arms stretching elegantly up towards the ceiling of the vast indoor rink. Her performance continued to be sharp throughout the whole routine. Although, Rochelle had not admired Rochelle's cropped haircut beforehand, it worked well on the ice with a wet-gelled look and an interesting hairpiece. Her bewitching, powder-blue costume was cutting-edge fashion. She looked trendy, and in actual fact, made the Canadian skater look a little old-fashioned in comparison.

Rochelle was relieved. The tension that she'd experienced before the performance began melted away as she witnessed the elation radiating from Vanessa. For one thrilling moment, the old Vanessa was back.

At the end of the slick performance, Vanessa burst into tears. Rochelle knew that her friend was weeping with tears of defiant joy.

She was buzzing with excitement as the blood rushed through her brain. She was grateful for the fact that there were two skaters before her. It would give her chance to calm her emotions and dry her tearful eyes. She knew that, for her to have any chance of winning a medal after Vanessa's skilful performance, she needed to pull off her spin faster than she'd ever managed before. She closed her eyes trying to regain some level of mental balance. At that moment, she heard the crowd erupt as Vanessa left the ice.

A short time later, it was Rochelle's turn to

be centre-stage on the ice. Remembering the first skater's imperfect posture, she stood tall and upright as she waited for the music to begin. At the first couple of beats to Whitney Houston's *'I Wanna Dance with Somebody,'* she glided across the ice. If she wanted to win a medal, she knew she needed to give the performance of her life.

The start of her program was astonishing. Wearing her corseted, silver costume, she glowed like a glimmering spark. Her costume alone was show stopping.

She continued to dazzle throughout her performance, showing off her incredible body. When she came to it, her spin was sensational, the diamantes on her costume glittering in the bright lights and reflection from the ice. The program was a little raunchy, and the crowd responded to it, applauding loudly. She oozed confidence and elegance as she burst into her jumps with enthusiasm. She was showing off, but she didn't care. Her dream was coming true. She wanted the highest prize.

As she dropped to the ice in her final pose, a hush came over the stadium before the crowd exploded into rapturous applause.

Juliet and Vanessa were both waiting for her

at the side of the rink. Through her tears, she could barely make out their faces.

"Bloody well done!" Vanessa screamed.

Rochelle's clammy hands were shaking.

"Wow! That's all I can say," Juliet said. "Just wow!"

Shaking all over, Rochelle couldn't speak, overwhelmed by the affection coming from the still ecstatic crowd. She was overjoyed with Juliet's reaction, but in the main, it was Vanessa's elation that really meant something to her.

"I always believed in you, I knew you could do it," she said, hugging Rochelle tightly.

"We're in this together, you and I. It was never going to be any different."

The camera lights dazzled around them as the photographers snapped shots of the two girls hugging one another. They blinked in the bright lights.

They turned to watch the final skater of their group. The girl skated with pace, precision, purpose and power. It was an exuberant performance, showcasing her abilities, but something was missing. She was unlikely to feature in the medals. She left the rink.

It was the end of their group … the time for all the scores to be added up. Rochelle was confident she would be in the top five, and believed Vanessa would be, too.

The scores were announced. Rochelle was in first place in the group, and Vanessa was in second. They exchanged hugs again, but knew they were still under pressure from the other 20 skaters.

After the ice had been cleaned, they watched the next group perform. The first three skaters offered no real competition, but the fourth was a strong contender, and there were 16 more girls yet to skate.

Vanessa placed her nervous hand in Rochelle's dear, familiar one, and they interlaced their fingers.

Rochelle's heart was thumping in her chest, and she bit the manicured, pink nails of her free hand. She almost couldn't bring herself to watch. She counted in her head; 16 more to go. With every stroke of the next skater's sharp blade, she squeezed Vanessa's tense, little hand even tighter.

At long last, the countdown was over, and all of the skaters had completed their first performance. She was placed second and Vanessa was fourth. Adrenaline rushed through her, as she worked out the relative scores. It was still possible for her to attain the gold and for Vanessa to take the silver or the bronze.

She rushed to the toilets, nausea overwhelming her once more.

Vanessa knocked the brown cubicle door.

"Are you okay?" she asked.

She sat on the toilet, unable to move.

"C'mon, Rochelle! We did well. We both have every chance of winning a medal."

Opening the cubicle door, she looked at Vanessa.

"It all sounds so simple in theory. But we have to do it all over again … only this time, even better!"

"It's our time! I know it! Anyway, we have no choice now. We just have to bring both medals home. The odds are on for you to win the gold, and I've every chance of getting at least the bronze."

"Yeah! But we could still end up being seventh or eighth."

"No! We'll get our rewards! We deserve it for all the effort we've put in."

Back in her quiet hotel room, Rochelle answered a polite knock at her door and was greeted by a uniformed bellboy, who handed her a massive bouquet of beautiful, exotic flowers, adorned with a dark pink ribbon tied in a bow.

"Are these for me?" she asked.

The bellboy handed them to her.

"Yes! It looks like you have an admirer," he said, and gave her a cheeky wink before he walked back down the corridor.

Her fingers fumbled with excitement, as she opened the attached envelope. She danced from foot to foot as she read words on the card:

'Well done, Beautiful! Christoph xxx'

After texting Christoph to say *'thank you'*, she called Gloria for a quick chat, following which, she had a few words with Derek. They were both full of praise for her.

She showered, ordered room service and climbed into bed feeling happy, but knowing that, if she wanted the gold, she had to remain sharp and focused. Christoph was skating in the men's short program the following day, and then it would be her turn for the free skate the day afterwards. There was still a mountain to climb, even though she was lying in the silver position.

As she closed her eyes and tried to sleep, she couldn't take her mind off Christoph.

She sent him a text message, which read: *"I can't sleep."*

CHAPTER 26

Five minutes later, a message flashed on Rochelle's phone screen. It was from Christoph.

It read: *'Me neither. Shall I come to your room?'*

Her heart slammed against her rib cage, and her fingertips hovered over her phone. If she said yes, it would be crossing the line of sensibility. They would probably jump into bed together and that would be unfair to him. He had his first competition tomorrow.

She texted back: *'I'm sorry. I shouldn't have texted you. You've got competitions tomorrow. Miss you! Hope you manage to get some sleep. Goodnight.'*

Reaching for the glass of water beside her bed, she regretted having sent her first text. She wouldn't blame him if he didn't reply now. She'd teased him, which had been unfair.

A frantic knock at Rochelle's bedroom door startled her. She opened it, expecting it to be Christoph, but was surprised to see Vanessa standing there.

"Let me in! Oh, Rochelle! I've been so stupid. They've just given me a random drugs test. I can't get disqualified! Not now!"

"When did you last take anything?"

"Four days ago … before we talked. I've not taken anything since. It had already dawned on me how stupid I've been."

Rochelle reached for her laptop.

"Let's Google it. See how long it stays in the system. Is it just MDMA you've taken? Anything else?"

"No! Only MDMA. Nothing else. I promise."

"It says here it lasts for up to 48 hours. It looks like you may have got away with it."

Vanessa bent down and picked something up off the floor.

"Look! A white feather! An angel must be watching over me. I'm never *ever* doing drugs again. Can you forgive me for almost ruining everything?"

"The white feather's from my mum. I see them all the time."

"I know! It's the angel's calling card."

"It's a sign from my mum to tell us to keep trusting faith, and to continue to stay strong."

"Your mum and dad – your real ones, I mean – would have been so proud of you today. The crowd went crazy. You're so popular, Rochelle."

"My stomach was in knots. It's all far more dramatic than I ever imagined. At least I've got Derek and Gloria here. I'm sorry your parents never made it out here to support you."

"Yeah! I guess their problems with each other were more important than me."

"It was tough today, but neither of us made any mistakes," Rochelle said.

"At the end of the day, it's as much about mental strength as it is physical strength."

"It's also about how much you want to win," Rochelle said.

"You deserve to be in second place, but you were so near to pinching the first."

"Yeah! The Canadian has always been the main favourite, though," Rochelle said.

"Do you remember when we first met? We were just eight years old. I'm so sorry that I've been so awful to you lately."

"Yes! I should yell and scream at you for all you've put me through. But there's no point."

"Well, I can honestly say that I felt happy and fulfilled again when I skated today," Vanessa said.

"I could tell. You skated with true inspiration. It came across in every move you made. It's why you scored as high as you did."

"Yes! No one can teach you that. It's either there, or it's not. Fortunately for us, it's who we are."

"We have to approach the next stage with confidence, and try not to be scared. Let's not allow even a shred of fear to enter our heads," Rochelle said.

The next day, Rochelle decided she would go and watch the men's short program competition. Christoph had texted her late last night, after Vanessa had left, saying *'Goodnight, Beautiful.'*

She took a seat in the corner of the skaters' families' enclosure, not wanting to mix, but keen to observe the competition and particularly Christoph's performance. She was so nervous for him, knowing he was not one of the favourites. There was a rush of energy around her as the first male competitor skated out to perform. In her opinion, he skated well, but he was nothing out of the ordinary. The second person to skate was good, but not brilliant. She was a little calmer as she watched the third skater achieve a perfect performance.

Fifteen minutes later, it was Christoph's turn. Rochelle focused her attention on her breathing, inhaling and exhaling slowly and deliberately as she tried to relax. The next five minutes were going to be agony for her.

As he skated out to the centre of the ice, she was full of admiration for him. Was this love? She couldn't wait to spend some time with him after the competitions. There was such a connection between them, as if she'd known him for years, not just days.

Tension overwhelmed her as she waited to hear his choice of music. Would it be classical or contemporary?

She was surprised by his opening passage,

which was charged with emotion and choreographed in a dramatic and ferocious manner. She was blown away. The music drove his performance, and it began to dawn on her that he could even stand a chance of winning a medal. He was having a magical time out there on the ice, and the large boisterous crowd were enthusiastically behind him.

Entering his final jump, she watched as he pulled his left shoulder back and down as far as possible to produce a show of pure, masculine power. His deft footwork was smooth, and the admirable combination resulted in a huge jump, which appeared effortless. It was a solid landing. He bowed to the judges looking cool, calm and collected. Oozing confidence, he skated off the ice.

Rochelle screamed with excitement, along with the rest of the crowd.

The next day was the big one for Rochelle. The main competition day! The day of truth!

She had woken from a night of unsettling dreams, but despite this, she was full of gratitude at being here to represent her country at the Winter Olympics.

Her competition wasn't due to start until 2 o'clock, so she met Derek and Gloria for breakfast in the hotel dining room. She was enveloped in a warm shower of good feelings, and she gave Derek and Gloria a huge smile as she greeted them. She felt truly relaxed in their company, laughing at Derek's jokes, even though she thought they were utterly pathetic.

"Is the coffee good, Dad?" she asked.

"Yes! Fabulous! Just like you," Derek responded with a smile.

"I'm glad we came out here to see you. I'm enjoying myself so much," Gloria said.

"You know, besides your natural talent for skating, what's got you here without a doubt, is your grit and determination. You should be proud of yourself," Derek told her, and took a sip of his steaming hot coffee.

"Passion and perseverance, as well," joined in Gloria.

"It's going to be difficult today, but I'm excited, and looking forward to it."

"If you make any mistakes, don't be too hard on yourself," Derek said. "You can only do your best."

"I guess I've not done too bad so far, all things considered. But my life has been an amazing adventure ever since you adopted me."

"You're a survivor, Rochelle! A strong and indomitable character," Gloria said.

"You've faced so much trauma. We can't tell you how proud we are of you," Derek added.

"The therapy helped … and your love, of course."

Gloria handed Rochelle a present.

"It's an aventurine crystal, given with our love for good luck. You'll always be our special little girl."

"Thank you both so much. You've done a great job of bringing me up, even if I say so myself."

Rochelle leant over the table and kissed them both in turn.

"The crystal's beautiful, but I don't need it for luck. My good luck began on the day you chose to make me your daughter."

A tear ran down her cheek. She wiped it away with the back of her hand.

As she looked up, she saw Christoph

approaching their table. He bent over and kissed her on both cheeks, in the customary Austrian way of greeting. Flushed, she introduced him to Derek and Gloria.

"Your girl's great," she heard him say.

"Would you like to join us?" Derek asked.

"I'd love to, but I'm afraid I've switched my preparatory training session to an early one, so that I can watch your beautiful daughter skate this afternoon."

Christoph turned and left the dining room. Rochelle watched through the dining room window as he left the hotel and walked through the torrent of fat snowflakes floating down from the pure white sky.

"I think that boy has a major crush on you," Gloria smiled.

"He seems to be a very nice young man," Derek joined in.

Rochelle was flustered, so she remained silent. The waitress brought over the bill, and Rochelle was grateful for the distraction. She picked up her gym bag and excused herself.

"I have to go and meet Juliet at the rink for a final practice. Love you. See you later."

Rochelle put her heart and soul into her final practice. Afterwards, Juliet stood back and applauded, even though at every jump she'd taken a sharp intake of icy breath, for fear of it resulting in even the slightest injury so close to the afternoon's competition.

"Splendid, Rochelle!" she said. "One hundred per cent splendid. Now let's get you off the ice. I can't take any more risks with you. My heart won't withstand it.."

Rochelle skated off the ice, a goofy smile fixed on her rosy-cheeked face.

"I'm confident you're going to do very well this afternoon," Juliet told her.

"Thank you, Juliet. I hope so."

"The audience will know that they are witnessing something very special when they see you skate today."

"Oh! Thank you! Thank you so much."

"You're welcome. You deserve all this praise."

Vanessa joined them.

"Hi! How's it going?'

"Great. Really good fun. How're you doing?" Rochelle asked.

"I've been *so* busy! I trained hard yesterday and again this morning."

"Are you excited about this afternoon?"

"Hell, yeah!"

"It's so important for us both to do our best," Rochelle said.

"It sure is!" Vanessa replied.

"We're an amazing combination, you and me! We always have been, ever since we first met," Rochelle said.

Vanessa gave Rochelle a hug.

"Yes! A pretty good one, I'd say."

"Go out and do your thing, Vanessa. Show them how good you really are."

"I've seen part of your routine, and I love it, Rochelle. Good luck for this afternoon! Go get that gold medal!"

CHAPTER 27

The final competition had commenced. The order of skating was determined by the position each skater had achieved in the short program. This meant that Vanessa and Rochelle had to wait until the final group of ten skaters. Vanessa, lying in fourth position, was to skate in 27th place, and Rochelle, lying in silver position, would be last but one, with only the Canadian girl left to skate after her.

She watched the first of the skaters perform their routines. While she did so, she willed herself to take the gold position from the Canadian girl.

Sitting beside her, Juliet said, "You've come a long way, Rochelle. And now this is it! Everything you've dreamt of and worked for."

Rochelle sighed.

"I know! All of my energy needs to go into this performance. Don't you think this girl's skating is a little bland, though?"

"Yes, she doesn't skate like you. You need to go out there and have fun … allow your mind to wander without constraint."

The next skater seemed to float across the ice. She was a vast improvement on the previous girl, Rochelle observed, but at a critical point, she made a clumsy mistake and fell.

Before Rochelle knew it, it was time for Vanessa to skate. Could she skate well enough to win the bronze medal? Juliet had been busy totalling the scores and the positions, and it was doable with the scores as they currently stood.

This was the biggest moment of Vanessa's life; she had trained innumerable hours for precisely this moment. She looked so young as she skated onto the ice. Her slight frame looked smaller than ever to Rochelle. She looked stylish, wearing a splendid black costume, which hugged her body attractively, and Rochelle noted the long, glossy black gloves covering her bare arms. She watched with apprehension as her friend smiled to her expectant fans, and she noted that she held a bold presence as she struck her pose in the middle of the rink.

Fidgeting in her hard seat, Rochelle tried to adjust herself into a more comfortable position. She inhaled, and then expelled all the air from her lungs. The anxiety was almost too much to bear. It was going to kill her to watch Vanessa's performance. She placed one trembling hand on her stomach and the other one on her chest to try and regulate the rise and fall.

Rochelle looked down at her own skates. She almost couldn't bring herself to look over at Vanessa, who was still waiting for her music to get under way. The delay was painful. She hoped there was nothing technically wrong, and they would get going soon.

Relief poured over her as Luciano Pavarotti's voice boomed out around the stadium. The blood pounded in Rochelle's ears. She took a long, deep gulp of air and dug her nails into her palms.

"Oh, fuck!" she muttered to herself, aware of Juliet beside her.

Vanessa skated her first steps, and although her movements were excellent, she appeared a little short of confidence.

But she soon stepped it up a gear. This was more like it, Rochelle thought, as Vanessa killed the first jump with style. She lunged into her first exquisite spin. She now appeared to inhabit a totally different physical realm; her skating was impressive as she performed another brilliantly dramatic jump.

Rochelle could tell that she was enjoying herself out there on the ice. The challenge for the bronze medal was on. She crossed her fingers. Vanessa couldn't lose it now.

One more agonising minute and it was all over, with only the slightest of mistakes.

The slim, 25-year-old French girl, who was lying in bronze position, skated out onto the ice wearing an elaborate, rose-gold costume.

She was popular. The huge audience cheered at the top of their voices. But Rochelle secretly hoped the girl wouldn't skate well to give Vanessa and herself a better chance.

Cher's *'If I Could Turn Back Time'* blared out, and Rochelle was shocked at her choice of music. She couldn't imagine for the life of her why the girl would have chosen this piece of music to skate to. The song had always annoyed her, and it was distracting her from the skating. Rochelle knew it wouldn't go well with the judges.

The girl's first jump wasn't executed well and she fell. After that, anything that might have given her an edge seemed to dribble out of her. Half way through her program, it began to look as though she wouldn't be finishing in the top three. It was sad to see that she'd fallen apart so badly, but Rochelle knew that a fall on your first jump often affected your nerves and shattered the rest of your performance.

Unfortunately, she'd lost the crowd, too; they were no longer behind her. The rest of her routine was just about okay.

Rochelle could see the agony that the girl was going through etched on her face, and although she felt sorry for her, it meant without doubt that Vanessa was going to waltz away with at least the bronze medal.

The girl misjudged her step into her final jump, and she fell again.

Rochelle, who was to skate next, hoped it wouldn't go so badly wrong for her. She just *had* to do better.

As she stood at the entrance of the rink waiting for her name to be announced, she wiped the sweat from her brow with a trembling hand.

Juliet smiled at her.

"Let's wrap this up and put a bow on it," she said.

With a beaming smile, Rochelle stepped onto the ice.

She'd come full circle.

This was her moment.

She could only be described as a glorious vision in deepest red as she skated to the centre of the rink. Her tasteful costume had it all, a sheer, glittering top and a low-cut back. It was, without question, gorgeous.

A silence fell over the domed stadium as Rochelle became lost in her own wonderful world of skating.

CHAPTER 28

Rochelle peered backwards over her shoulder as she waited for the first beat of her music. Her hair was in a half-up, half-down style with glamorous curls tumbling down her back.

Her opening was phenomenal. Her chemistry with the ice was unreal.

Her first jump was explosive as she powered all her energy into it.

Confidence oozed from her, her first spin, strong.

The audience was fascinated.

The pressure was on for the gold medal.

The next few minutes would determine whether her dreams would come true, whether her efforts had all been worth it.

Her timing was at one with the beat of the

captivating music. Even her basic steps were performed to absolute perfection and in time. She was transported into her own beautiful world of skating, oblivious to the large crowd and the magnitude of the occasion. She was expressing her emotions through her movements … a true master of the perfect careful timing.

The mighty roar of the exuberant crowd was growing louder. She had them right where she wanted them. They were showing her their wholehearted support, and Rochelle was giving them a spectacular show.

Coldplay's *'White Shadows'* echoed its pleasing tune and clever lyrics around the indoor stadium, and Rochelle's imaginative interpretation of the track was magnificent.

She could have been a ballet dancer, such was the elegance of her skating. Her slight frame, precise movements and her graceful, flowing arms were a delight to watch. She was excelling. She was in her prime.

The audience went crazy as her performance came to a close. Her commitment had paid off and she beamed at the crowd.

As she skated off the ice, it was as though she'd lived this moment many times before. It had been her dream for so long.

Juliet greeted her with a hug.

"Well, blow me away, why don't you!"

With that performance, the competition had all changed. Rochelle was now a clear contender for the gold. The final skater would have to pull out all the stops to win.

Rochelle watched as the Canadian skated onto the ice, the audience applauding as if to wake the dead. Luck, as well as talent, would need to be on this skater's side.

Her opening was an ultra big jump, which she landed with precision. Her style was elegant. Her first spin was insane.

She was living her moment, sharing her experience with the crowd. It was beautiful to watch. Her love for skating shone through. She made it look easy.

CHAPTER 29

Rochelle's adrenaline was skyrocketing as she continued to watch the Canadian skater. She had no control over what would happen next. The gold medal rested on the remainder of this skater's performance. She glanced at Juliet, but her eyes were transfixed on the ice, watching the girl intently. Rochelle's head felt as though it was about to burst.

Doubt, envy and fear hit her all at once.

With only a minute left of her programme, it happened. As the girl landed a triple jump, her knee buckled.

"Oh, my God!" Juliet screamed. "Looks like an anterior cruciate ligament injury from here."

The Canadian skater limped off the ice in agony, bitter tears telling the story of her shattered dreams.

"Poor girl! It's a horrible injury, isn't it?" Rochelle said, forgetting for the present moment that it meant just one thing: she had secured the gold and Vanessa had won the silver.

Juliet hugged Rochelle.

"You've done it! You've taken the gold! All the effort you've put in has paid off."

Tears of joy sprung from Rochelle's eyes as she threw her arms in the air. Vanessa was running towards her, arms outstretched. As they spun each other around in excited circles, Rochelle spotted Derek and Gloria rushing towards them, their faces full of pride and Gloria in tears.

It was difficult for Rochelle to comprehend it all. It was going to take time for it all to sink in. The dream had come true, but she was aware it had partly been down to the Canadian girl's misfortune. Luck had been a huge factor, as well as talent, but she wasn't going to let it spoil the occasion. It was the most amazing day of her life.

Standing on top of the podium, Rochelle waved at the crowds, a huge smile spreading across her face. Her childhood dream had been spot on … the dream where the gold medal was placed around her neck while the British National Anthem rung out and a Union Jack was raised to denote both her gold, and Vanessa's silver, achievement.

On this occasion, it was the Canadian flag that was flying a little lower for the bronze position. Vanessa giggled at her side, struggling to contain her excitement.

Back in the hotel, the British team celebrated Rochelle and Vanessa's success. The champagne was free-flowing, and a pianist played uplifting tunes at the grand piano.

Rochelle grinned as she saw Christoph walking in her direction.

"Gold! You did it!"

He bent in towards her and kissed her full on the lips in front of the whole room. As they finally let go of each other, her face reddened as she realised that everyone was clapping them.

Derek handed her another glass of champagne.

"Congratulations, Rochelle! And it looks as though you haven't just won the championship, but this young man's heart as well."

Christoph led her to a couple of bar stools next to the grand piano. Something about the champagne, the headiness of the whole magical day and Christoph's amorous public kiss suddenly caused her to giggle.

He whispered in her ear.

"You're turning me into a quivering heap. You're so irresistible."

She gazed into his enigmatic eyes, which were full of warm affection, and her giggles changed to a broad happy smile.

"You're pretty handsome, yourself."

"Never stop kissing me. I want you to kiss me until we're old and grey."

Rochelle ran a hand through her hair, as Juliet approached them.

"Thank you for helping me to achieve my dream. It's pretty amazing what you've done for me," Rochelle said.

"What are your plans now? Are you going to glitter in the limelight, or go and hide somewhere away from it all?" Juliet enquired.

"I have to admit, I don't want the limelight. It was never the reason I wanted to win."

"I'm hoping to offer her some sanctuary," Christoph butted in. "I'm hoping to persuade Rochelle to come away with me for a while after my finals tomorrow – somewhere peaceful and quiet – and, afterwards, I'm hoping she'll come and spend some time at my home in Austria, whilst she decides what she wants to do with her immediate future."

A sudden rush of gratitude overcame Rochelle.

"Oh! Christoph, I'd love to."

Vanessa came over, and the four of them shared an enthusiastic group hug, slapping high-fives all around.

"I want to remember this long-anticipated day of victory forever," she said.

"I'm afraid I'm going to have to leave you guys to celebrate without me. I need to rest now for my finals tomorrow," Christoph said. He kissed Rochelle goodnight.

"Yeah! Sure! Good luck for tomorrow. I'll

be there to watch. You've every chance of stealing the bronze," Rochelle said. "Just go for it."

As Christoph left, Gloria came over to Rochelle and gave both her and Vanessa a hug.

"I'm so proud of you both," she said.

Drying an impromptu tear from her eye, Rochelle hugged Gloria as tightly as she could, remembering again how lucky she'd been to be adopted by such loving and caring parents. There was still a void – a sadness – surrounding her real parents and Lloyd, but she loved Derek and Gloria, and she had possibly fallen in love with Christoph.

The following day, Rochelle sat with Gloria and Derek waiting for Christoph's turn to skate. She stiffened in her seat as she noticed the television cameras had turned their attention on her, presumably to watch her reaction to his name being announced. She placed her clenched hands underneath her slender thighs, not sure what to do with them.

It seemed an eternity before he skated out on to the ice and when he finally did, she pumped her right fist into the air.

Rochelle knew the ambitious programme Christoph was about to skate was risky. If he pulled it off, it would be hugely worth it, but there was an awful lot that could go wrong. She thrust her shaking hands into her armpits and shuddered. It would be very difficult to watch. But, just in case the cameras panned back in again to record her reaction, she kept a forced smile on her face, her top row of teeth showing, and a faint curve to her lips. There was no crease below her eyes, though, and no upward movement of her cheeks.

A sudden buzz of excitement flew around the stadium, and blood rushed to her brain. It was show time: the final three male skaters, all of them in their prime.

The music began: Jackie Wilson, *'Your Love Keeps Lifting Me Higher'*. It was one of Rochelle's favourite tracks.

Christoph's skating opened with passion, as he headed straight into a classic spiral spin. The jumps that followed were explosive, and he landed them with precision. The result was thrilling to watch.

He was an extraordinary skater, and the risks he was taking were paying off.

CHAPTER 30

Rochelle and Christoph were sitting together in the hotel bar. He'd taken the bronze medal and was as thrilled with his achievement as she was with hers.

"If we were alone now, I'm not sure you'd be able to trust me not to make a move on you," Christoph said.

She blushed, as her mind became lost in the fantasy.

"Our lives have changed so much. I still can't believe what's happened."

"Do you want to join me on the journey I mentioned? We could leave as early as tomorrow? Unless you want to stay for the closing ceremony?"

"I don't want to stay. I want to get away from the prying eyes of the press as soon as possible. Yes, Christoph! I'd love to come with you."

Her skin tingled as she took in his slim but muscular frame.

He handed her a little gift bag.

"A small present to say, 'well done'. I hope you like it."

Hands shaking, she opened the bag. Perfume … he'd bought her perfume.

"It's called Epic Woman! Rather fitting, I'd say."

Removing the top, she sprayed a little onto her wrists and breathed it in.

"Oh, Christoph! It's gorgeous. I love it." She leaned over and kissed him on the cheek. "Thank you."

"I love skating, but I must admit I can't wait not to have to do it every single day for the rest of my life," Christoph said.

"I know! I'm the same. Be nice to do it only for pleasure now … whenever I get the urge."

"It'll be nice to have some time to do exactly as we please."

"Yes! In actual fact, I don't know what I want to do in the future, but it'll be nice to get away and have a little break to think about it all."

"Where would you like to go?"

"I've always wanted to go to Amsterdam. I want to see Anne Frank's house."

"Amsterdam it is, then. Shall I see if I can get flights for tomorrow?"

"Tomorrow would be great. I can't believe we're doing this."

The following day was an emotional one for Rochelle … saying a painful goodbye to Derek and Gloria … not knowing when she'd see them next. They'd had a nice lunch together and she was now en route to the airport, with Christoph, her stomach in knots as her thoughts drifted back to the comfortable, stable home they'd given her, and all the love they'd showered upon her over the years.

"I'm determined to make the most of every second of my life. My parents had their lives taken from them when they were still so young," Rochelle said.

"Yeah! I'm the same. It makes you want to live every day as if it's your last," Christoph said.

"When we get to the airport, I want to buy a journal and start keeping a day-to-day record of what we do together. I want to make sure I remember it all."

"You're so beautiful, Rochelle. I'm so happy we're going to be able to spend some time together."

Their taxi pulled up at the drop-off point for the airport. After checking-in, clearing security and purchasing Rochelle's journal, they found somewhere to sit down for a coffee.

"I'm going to miss Vanessa. She's been such a big part of my life up to now. I hope she's gonna be okay. She's got a good deal with Disney on Ice, so her future's pretty secure."

A warm smile spread over Christoph's face.

"It's not like you're never going to see her again. I'm sure you'll be chatting on the phone whenever you get the slightest opportunity."

"I'm so glad I met you. I can't wait for this new chapter of my life to begin."

"You're the best thing that's happened to me in a long while," he said, leaning across the table to squeeze her hand.

A sense of quiet calm overcame her as she

gazed into his eyes.

Amsterdam was everything she'd dreamed of and more. Christoph had taken care of all the details and had sorted an apartment for them to rent for a week. She was pleased it had two bedrooms. Even though she wanted to share a bed with him, she was relieved he hadn't put her under any pressure to do so.

That evening, they arrived at the restaurant called The City Street Kitchen, which he'd booked earlier in the day. They were led to a table on the rooftop terrace, and although the evening was cold, she felt warm sitting under the outdoor heater, wrapped in the cosy blanket the waiter had provided. She had no idea which part of Amsterdam they were in, but the view of the city and its canals was fantastic. Their food was served, and it was delicious.

"This is so awesome. Thank you for sorting all this out," she said.

"I'm so happy to share it with you. By the way, you look stunning, Rochelle. The dress looks fabulous on you."

"I still can't believe you bought it for me, and even managed to get the size right. It fits to absolute perfection. It must have cost you a fortune."

"In truth, money isn't an issue for me. I was left a substantial inheritance by my parents."

"You can't keep spending it on me though," she laughed.

"A bottle of perfume and a dress! It's nothing! Anyway, orange definitely suits you."

"Can we go to Anne Frank's house tomorrow?"

"Yes, of course! And afterwards, I would like to take you shopping. I want to spoil you. I can afford it, so allow me to please."

He leaned across the table and planted a kiss on her lips.

The elderly, English-speaking waiter brought over their desserts, and Rochelle tucked into the sweet, gooey chocolate ice cream she'd ordered.

Christoph winked at Rochelle.

"This cake is amazing. Here try some," he said, scooping a large piece onto his spoon and guiding it carefully into her mouth.

She licked her lips and closed her eyes.

"Oh my goodness!" she said. "That is *so*

good!"

Pushing the dish containing her last bit of ice cream away from her, she said, "I can't eat another mouthful. I'm fit to burst."

"Are you tired yet?"

"Yes! I'm shattered. Shall we call it a night?"

"Sure," he said, and summoned the waiter to bring over the bill.

Turning the key to their spacious ornate apartment, he said, "Our nice, old-fashioned, but splendid, home for the entire week!"

As they entered, the world rushed by in a blur as she fell into the security of his strong arms. She kissed him with a violent passion, their tongues exploring each other's mouths. His sensitive fingers caressed the top of her cleavage, which was showing a little at the front of her flattering dress. He picked her up and carried her to his bed, placing her on top of its silky-soft duvet as they continued their kiss.

The following day was filled with breath-taking views and romantic history. Amsterdam had an elegant, yet laid-back,

297

playful vibe. It was the perfect setting for their budding romance to flourish.

The weather was kind to them, the high-unclouded sun shining for most of the day. After visiting Anne Frank's dark and quiet house, they took a pleasant stroll through the narrow, cobbled streets and magical little alleyways, stopping from time to time for a hot spiced coffee in one of the many adorable smoky cafes. She declined his offer of shopping for her, stating he'd already spent more on her than he should have done. To Rochelle, it was as though she was living in a fairy tale, as they crossed the charming bridges over the enchanting, sleepy canals.

Back at the apartment getting ready to go out for the evening, she took in the sheer luxury of the place. The two bedrooms interconnected, and although she hadn't slept in her own room the night before, she was pleased to have the privacy of her own bathroom. The rainfall shower was delightful and she stayed underneath it for longer than she intended.

Being on the 14th floor meant that they had great views of the city from the floor to ceiling windows. The lounge area had a large, curved sofa and a TV, which was bigger than any she'd ever seen before. The amount of clothes she had with her looked pitiful in the over-sized, walk-in wardrobe. Maybe she should have let him take her shopping after all? She questioned herself as she applied her make-up.

Tonight's venue was a tiny trattoria.

"I hope you enjoy Italian food – it's my favourite. We might be in Amsterdam, but you can't beat a good Italian," he said.

The tables were covered with snow-white tablecloths. On being seated, the waiter handed her a menu. It was extensive. As she browsed it, Christoph's question took her by surprise.

"Do you ever ask yourself why your real parents named you Rochelle?"

"No! Not until now, that is," she answered truthfully.

"It's actually a big decision – the name you give to a tiny baby."

"Yeah! I guess so. It's something they've given me for life. Something to hold on to. It's quite a comforting thought."

"I like the way you've done your hair tonight – tied up in a ponytail like that. It suits you.

It's sort of sweet, but seductive, at the same time."

"Thank you," she took a sip of the fine claret he'd ordered. "You know, it's only just sinking in that we both won medals. To tell the truth, I'm still uncertain about what I want to do with my future though."

"Yeah! Me too. I'm definitely going to take a year out before I decide, though, and I'm hoping you'll come and travel with me."

"I guess we both need time to reinvent ourselves. Skating has been our lives for so long."

"Well, that's certainly true. But you also need to remember what you've achieved. An Olympic gold medal! Your real parents must be looking down on you with such pride."

"I guess I did it for them, too, to some extent. Do *you* want children at some point in your life, Christoph?"

"I'm longing to have kids, but it has to be with the right person at the right time."

"I was so young when they died. I hardly have any memories of them."

"Well, we both deserve a bit of fun in our lives now, and I'm determined to make sure we have some."

"You always know how to make me smile. I've never felt safer or more comfortable than I do when I'm with you."

After a delicious dinner, they strolled, hand in hand, alongside one of the smaller, quaint canals. It was an oasis of calm in the cultural centre of Amsterdam. A beam of silver moonlight shone across the opaque water, adding an air of magic to the setting.

"So where shall we go after Amsterdam?" Christoph asked.

"The choice should be yours, as I chose to come here."

"I'm glad you said that. I'm thinking of somewhere a little more exotic than here. What would you say to Southeast Asia? We could start off in Malaysia and see where we go from there."

"Wow! How exciting! I'd have never dreamed of going somewhere so far away."

"Great! I'll sort it all out then."

"Will it be hot? I've only got winter clothes with me."

"Then you'll have to agree to the shopping trip I wanted to take you on. It's now a necessity."

The following day, Christoph treated her to the shopping trip of her lifetime. He was determined to spoil her, and she had great fun allowing him to do so. Money had always been a little tight with Gloria and Derek, her skating having taken so much of their modest budget. New clothes had always been seen as a bit of a luxury. Shopping with Christoph was completely different, as he told her not to look at the price tags, but to choose whatever she liked. He helped to make her choices, though, and encouraged her to buy many more items than she'd intended.

Back at the fancy, two-bedroomed apartment, she laid out all of the purchases on the large bed: 9 dresses, 5 pairs of skimpy shorts, 7 cool tops, 2 fine, silk nighties, 3 pairs of pretty sandals, and 3 bikinis. She had never been so spoiled in her life, and what made it extra-special was how apparent it was that Christoph had taken such pleasure in the whole experience.

As she dressed in her tightest white jeans and cutest red jumper for tonight's exhilarating adventure, she wondered what the guided walking tour of Amsterdam, named the 'naughty tour', would involve.

They met their guide at a museum dedicated to prostitution, which if truth be known, she found interesting and informative. It gave her a better understanding of why and how beautiful young girls became involved in the illicit trade. When she thought about it, she was even more grateful to Derek and Gloria for rescuing her from the inefficient care system, which resulted in so many girls being forced to turn to prostitution, after leaving their children's home with precious few options available to them. She made a mental note to call them tomorrow and let them know what a fabulous time she was having.

She turned to Christoph.

"It's been an amazing experience so far."

"Yeah! A 'once in a life time' one! I believe we are off to the Red Light District next, and then to a sex show. I hope you won't get offended."

"Quite the opposite!" she said. "I've learned so much already. I'm finding the tour guide, and the tour itself, totally fascinating."

A few days later they boarded a Boeing 787 headed for Kuala Lumpur. It was Rochelle's first time aboard a long-haul flight, and she was struggling to contain her excitement.

She was like a rational adult and an adventurous child all rolled into one, as she sipped the ice-cold champagne she'd been handed by the air stewardess.

Their breakfast was served a short time after take-off, and as Rochelle glanced over at Christoph in the next seat, it dawned on her that she wanted to eat breakfast with him as many times as she could. Again, she asked herself whether she had fallen in love.

As the breakfast trays were removed, he placed his strong arm around her, and she cuddled into him. Then, she gradually drifted off into a restful sleep feeling more content than at any other time in her life.

Woken by a sudden charge of sexuality surging through her body, she met Christoph's deep-set brown eyes. Realising that he had been watching her sleep, she blushed. He bent in and kissed her on her soft, flirtatious lips.

"You look even more beautiful when you're asleep," he whispered.

In response, her fingers caressed his muscular bicep, which extended beyond the sleeve of his t-shirt.

The flight passed speedily as they exchanged secrets about their childhood and skating careers.

"Skating was always good for me in so many ways," she said.

"It was the same for me once, but … I don't know … in the last few months of training, I've lost the magic somewhere," Christoph said.

"I guess when we reached the level we did, it all became a bit scary."

"I got so fed up of hearing other people's opinions on my skating," he said.

"It definitely got harder when so many of us were all after the same goal."

Having arrived at Kuala Lumpur airport, which looked more like a shopping mall than Rochelle had expected, they collected their luggage and headed for the immense arrivals lounge where Christoph informed Rochelle a driver would be waiting to meet them. Sure enough, at the entrance, a beautiful, young lady in a jet-black dress stood holding a plaque with Christoph's name on it, ready to escort them to their sleek, foreign car.

Kuala Lumpur took Rochelle completely by surprise, and the drive towards the city was not at all what she'd expected. The car had a pleasant, new car smell, the roads were smooth and well maintained, and the city was far more affluent-looking than she'd imagined. Beethoven's 6th blared from the radio as Christoph took hold of her hand and squeezed it. It was all so exciting.

No one knew her here, and that knowledge relaxed her. She opened her handbag, double-checking that she'd placed her journal inside it. She couldn't wait to write in it, now that they'd arrived in Malaysia. Amsterdam had been a blast, but this was something altogether different. Even the trees at the side of the roads looked unusual. There were species she'd never seen in her life before.

She leaned over and kissed Christoph on the cheek.

"Thank you. I feel so lucky," she whispered.

CHAPTER 31

The hotel suite Christoph had booked for them was amazing. After the bellboy had delivered their cases, Christoph pulled Rochelle towards him on the huge, richly-upholstered armchair. Placing his hand inside her blouse, he stimulated her already aroused nipple, stroking her hair with his other hand.

"You're so hot, Rochelle! I can't keep my hands off you."

"It's been a long day. Shall I run a bath for us to share?"

Climbing into the foamy bath water, she sat between his legs and leaned her back into the safe haven of his chest. He pulled her closer to him and caressed her body with his soapy hands.

They rose at daybreak. Christoph had booked them a golf lesson at the nearby course. Neither of them had ever played before, and they'd agreed that it would be great fun to try their hands at a sport other than skating.

As Rochelle watched Christoph attempting his first wide swings of the club, a warm, fuzzy sensation overcame her, and her heart skipped a beat. She was becoming increasingly aware of the close connection forming between them.

He was picking up the popular game like a natural, and she shouted over, "Well done! Great shot!"

That evening, they found themselves in an Irish bar that had been recommended to them as a great venue for a fun night out. It was apparently 'the place to go'. Christoph had ordered them both a pint of Guinness. Rochelle wasn't too sure about the taste, having never drunk it before, but she tried not to show her distaste as she took another large gulp of the dark brown liquid.

Sitting outside on the terrace, they were still able to hear each other speak over the strains of Irish folk music being played inside the bar by a traditional Irish band. Looking over at Christoph, she was so grateful for how happy he was making her feel.

Whilst he went to the bar to order more drinks, Rochelle leant back in her chair and listened to the people around her talking and laughing. The evening was hot and humid, and the sounds of the city traffic blared past the smart terrace, which had been transformed into a mini garden with seating areas all around.

She was so alive – totally free from her old life. The sky was a deep indigo in this bustling, energetic city that she'd already fallen in love with. The city lights from the surrounding buildings twinkled and enchanted her.

After they'd finished their next drinks, Christoph suggested they order room service back at their hotel and have a romantic, candle-lit dinner together.

Later, putting on her scant, silk nightie and lying next to Christoph with her feet draped over his lap, Rochelle felt calm and content. The beautiful suite was perfect in every way.

Christoph had selected a Beatles album on the sound system, and Rochelle smiled at him as the first few rhythmic beats of *'All You Need Is Love'* bounced off the walls of the comfortable, lavish room.

With jetlag setting in, she closed her eyes, the soothing, blue décor of the lounge calming her mind.

He whispered into her ear, "To me, you are perfect."

He pulled her up gently towards him and lay her head between his chest and shoulders so that he could plant a kiss on her forehead.

The following morning, Christoph had arranged for a guide and driver to collect them from the hotel. They headed away from the city down long, narrow, winding roads towards ancient sites and famous landmarks. As they looked around, their guide, Mahmud, made the past come alive with his many tales of historical happenings.

Skinny dogs surrounded them, and Mahmud tried to usher them away, but against his advice Rochelle wanted to fuss them. A man was selling a few items from his stall. There were very few tourists around, so Rochelle bought a beaded necklace and told him to keep the change. It was handmade and she saw his pride when she told him how beautiful it was, and that he was selling it for far too low a price. Mahmud laughed and said she should be haggling to bring the price down, not to pay more.

Turning to Rochelle, Christoph said, "I think I've fallen in love with you."

In divine unison with his words, a spectacular lightning show illuminated the heavens. Dense, turbulent clouds formed, and distant thunderclaps rolled across the stormy sky. Mahmud gestured for them to return to the safety of their car, where their driver was waiting for them.

"I don't know which shook me more – your words or the sudden bright flashes of lightning, 'Rochelle laughed.

"Do you know that you count the seconds between the flash of lightning and the clap of thunder to work out how far you are from the eye of the storm?" Christoph asked.

"Yeah! Derek taught me that. It's five seconds for every mile."

They arrived at their next hotel in one of the oldest towns of Malaysia. The room was cute and swanky.

"It's a trendy, art hotel. I hope you like it," Christoph said.

She smiled at him. He did have impeccable taste, and she appreciated the fact that he was sorting everything out for her, including booking the beautiful hotels in advance. He was also more than willing to pay for everything, although she was contributing whenever she could.

The exclusive hotel was unique, and she loved it. It was all so chic. The breath-taking, panoramic views from their single, shuttered window were incredible. They were surrounded by fertile hills and mountains, but the hotel was in the heart of a small town.

She lay on the comfortable bed, kicked off her sensible, flat shoes, and melted into the huge, soft pillow, listening to the sounds of the busy nightlife outside.

"I've booked us into the spa late tomorrow morning," Christoph said.

"Fantastic," she replied enthusiastically. "Shall we rest for a little while now, and afterwards head into town for dinner?"

An hour later, Rochelle chose one of the

dresses Christoph had bought her and slipped it over her head.

"I'm ready," she said, as she applied some lip balm to her lips.

The storm had passed, and they walked along the riverbank until they stumbled upon a bar serving cocktails. As they sipped at their drinks, they watched exotic-coloured birds flying gracefully across the river.

Later, they had dinner on the balcony of a restaurant situated further along the riverbank. Afterwards, they strolled at a snail's pace back to their hotel. On their return, Rochelle floated into a blissful sleep.

After a healthy, open-air breakfast, they headed for the spa. Rochelle baulked at the price of the treatments on the menu that the lady at the spa was offering her.

"Choose whatever you fancy." Christoph said.

This was an interesting experience for Rochelle, who'd never set foot inside a spa before. It took her a long time to read the descriptions of the treatments on offer, trying to forget about the high prices shown next to them.

"I'd like something relaxing," she said as her senses were soothed with the fragrance of jasmine.

The lady offered her a refreshing wet towel and a fruit juice.

"Take your time. There's no rush," she said.

Rochelle chose a hot stone massage, and as the masseuse worked away at the knots in her back, her mind drifted to Christoph ... back to the first time he had kissed her and how her world had exploded since then. All at once, she was hit by the realisation that she was indeed in love with him.

She wanted to show him her appreciation and gratitude for all he had done for her. Saying thank you was not enough, but what could she do? It needed to be something memorable ... something he would always remember in the fondest of ways ... something adventurous. She didn't want it to involve food. He had already taken her to some amazing restaurants. This would need to be something completely different.

The deep massage over, the masseuse led Rochelle to the relaxation area, where some magazines and newspapers lay on the table at the side of her reclining chair. She picked up a British tabloid and her brain stuttered in shock for a moment to see a black and white photograph of herself and Christoph dominating the front page with the headline, *'Gold medal for Rochelle, but will a gold ring be next?'*.

The photograph was of them both at the Irish bar in Kuala Lumpur.

Horrified, Rochelle read on.

The Olympian was spotted with Christoph, the Austrian bronze medalist, in an Irish bar in Malaysia, letting her hair down on a well-deserved holiday. Rochelle Erickson looked relaxed and happy in the company of her handsome young companion. Are wedding bells about to chime?'

She was mortified. What would Christoph make of it all? Without the slightest delay, she hid the newspaper deep underneath the other papers on the table.

By the time Christoph joined her, she had fully recovered from discovering the devastating newspaper article and was lying back in her comfortable reclining chair, doing exactly what she was supposed to be doing in the luxurious relaxation area … relaxing.

She realised that this was another romantic

setting away from her usual, day-to-day grind. Her life was once more like living in a fairy tale, the peace and quiet of the remote spa alleviating any concerns or worries she may have.

After half an hour, they were led to a charming tearoom and were served with a hearty afternoon tea. He'd done it again – spoiled her rotten – and she beamed at him as they indulged in golden-crusted scones with thick clotted cream and delicious jam, dainty finger sandwiches, assorted cream cakes and a drink of loose-leaf, herbal tea poured from a ceramic green teapot into white, bone china cups and saucers.

The couple on the next table caught Rochelle's eye. They appeared to be talking about her and Christoph.

The woman piped up, "Hello! Aren't you Rochelle Erickson, the skater?"

"Oh, hi! Yes! I am," Rochelle replied.

"Well, it's charming to meet you. My husband and I are English. We watched you win the gold on the telly. We were so proud."

Rochelle blushed.

"Thank you. That's kind of you to say."

"I'm Melinda, and this is my husband, Greg."

She glanced over at Christoph.

"Oh, and you're the Austrian skater, Christoph, aren't you?"

Christoph grinned.

"Yes! I'm the Austrian one."

"Your parents must all be so proud of you," she continued.

"Yes! They are," Rochelle, replied, unwilling to divulge any of her own or Christoph's private affairs.

"Well, we shouldn't interfere with your day. I'm sorry to have imposed on you both."

"Not at all," Christoph said. "We're happy to share some company."

Melinda chuckled, "Wait till I tell my friends back home that I sat on the next table to you at the spa, and I even spoke to you."

"I'm only a skater," Rochelle stated.

"Well, I can tell you I'm thrilled," Melinda said, as she leaned over and rubbed Rochelle's arm with her outstretched hand.

Startled, Rochelle instinctively moved further away, shrinking into her seat.

"Excuse me," Rochelle said. "We have to leave. We've a prior engagement, and we can't be late."

Back in the privacy of their room, Christoph asked, "Would you like to explain to me why we left like we did?"

Rochelle ran her fingers over the figured silk wall covering.

"I'm sorry. I know it was rude, but this is why I almost wish I hadn't won the gold medal. I don't want that type of attention."

CHAPTER 32

The more Rochelle and Christoph travelled, the more she learned about the diversity of the world and how different people lived their lives.

They were six months into their travelling and had visited four continents. Rochelle had decided that whatever she was going to do careerwise would involve trying to make a difference in the lives of people less fortunate than herself, but she hadn't quite narrowed it down yet.

Today, they'd arrived at the lost city of Petra, in Jordan. Their hotel was a short drive away from the airport, and it was, as usual, stunningly beautiful, located at the summit of a spectacular mountain range. The city itself was enchanting … luring the visitor in, to unravel its many secrets. It was a magnificent sight. The Bedouin riders on their horses intrigued her. The effect they had as they galloped past was mesmerising.

Christoph took Rochelle's hand as they ambled along the stony paths. A sense of pure bliss overcame her as she gazed into his eyes when he bent down and kissed her forehead. It was a truly intimate moment. It still seemed like she was living in a fairy tale.

They entered a cave to observe how Bedouin families lived and then hiked on further down the path, exploring the different colours of the sandstones.

Rochelle took so many photos she was worried that her memory card would soon be full. She had never seen such unspoiled natural beauty in her life. Petra was inspiring her in ways she did not understand. It was magical and mystical. She clutched her camera and snapped some more shots trying to capture the soul of this wonderful place.

Back at the hotel, they spent a relaxed afternoon by the swimming pool. Rochelle read a book, listened to some music and then closed her eyes and fell asleep in the heat of the afternoon sun.

The ringing of her mobile phone woke her.

'Gloria would like face time' flashed across the screen. She accepted the call. Gloria's face appeared with Derek standing behind her.

"Rochelle, we love you. We're missing you *so* much. Are you okay?" Gloria asked.

"I love you both back. Yeah! I'm good thanks."

"We can't wait to see you in Austria next month. It's so kind of Christoph to have invited us to stay at his house. Is he okay? Is he there with you?" Gloria asked.

"He's in the pool, having a swim. Yeah! I can't wait either. I'm *so* looking forward to seeing where he lives, and I can't wait to see you both, either. It'll be nice to be settled in one place for a while. The travelling's been fantastic, but I'm ready to settle down for a bit now. I need to decide what I want to do workwise, too."

Rochelle squinted against the hot afternoon sun.

"Bear with me a minute. I'm gonna move into the shade. I can't see you very clearly with this blinding glare on my screen."

"What time is it there, love?" Derek asked.

"It's five. We'll stay here until about six, and

then shower and change ready for dinner."

"What can we get Christoph as a thank you for inviting us over?" Gloria asked.

"There's a book he mentioned he wanted to get. I'll send the details over to you."

"I'm counting the days now. It's 22 to be precise until we see you," Gloria said.

"Yay! We're going to be at Christoph's in six days' time. Mum, hold the phone up a bit higher. I can't see you."

"So, what's it like in Jordan?" Derek asked.

"After all the fantastic places we've visited, I didn't expect to be so blown away by Petra. It's spellbinding."

"Is the hotel nice?" Gloria asked.

"Very peaceful. We've had the pool to ourselves all afternoon. The interior's really posh; more or less everything is white."

"So … you mentioned earlier about finding work once you've settled down. Is there anything in particular you'd like to do?" Derek asked.

"Yeah! I've narrowed it down a bit. I want to get involved in the battle against human trafficking, but I'm not sure exactly how I can do that yet."

"Well, it would certainly be a worthwhile occupation," Derek said.

The following morning, Rochelle and Christoph awoke to a cloudless sky. Their plan was to go mountain biking. They'd done it a few times during their travels, and although it was demanding for Rochelle to try and keep up with Christoph, she found the whole experience exhilarating.

In reality, though, even though she was still relishing every moment of their travels, she was really looking forward to settling down in Austria, and also to researching the sort of role she could play in combatting the escalating human trafficking trade.

Dropping their bikes to the ground, they sat down beside a lake. The sun scorched their faces as they watched the light dancing on the water. Rochelle took in the beauty of the moment. Jordan was the most amazing country.

Despite wearing her sunglasses, she squinted, as she glanced over at Christoph, she noted his bronzed skin from the months of travelling. She loved him so much, and for a fleeting second, a sense of panic overtook her at the thought of losing him like she had her parents and Lloyd. But she checked herself. It couldn't possibly happen again.

A bold Billy goat moved towards them, the rest of his pack following more nervously behind.

The manager of the hotel had invited Rochelle and Christoph to a party on the evening. It was to be an exclusive event for some top officials who were visiting Petra.

Rochelle took extra care when getting ready, as she wanted Christoph to be proud of her. Looking through her wardrobe, she scratched her head, uncertain what to wear. It was a cocktail event, so she wanted to look both elegant and respectful of their local culture. In the end, she decided on a high-necked, red silk dress, which was cut below her knees. She'd only worn it once before, and Christoph had particularly admired it. It was one he had chosen for her on one of their shopping trips. She elevated her look with jewellery and a pair of red strappy heels.

The balcony overlooking the swimming pool was *the* most romantic setting for the party, with views that were beyond magical. Their host, Salah, greeted them in his charming style. Her life had been transformed, and she stood oozing perfect confidence amongst the international dignitaries who were being entertained at tonight's event.

Her travels had shifted her mind into a healthy, rational place. She had never been happier. The love, companionship and adventures she'd shared with Christoph were beyond anything she could have envisaged. It was as though her Fairy Godmother had waved her magic wand over her, just like in the story of Cinderella. She took a minute to take in the exquisite beauty of everything around her. Without question, she would have a lot to write in her journal about Jordan.

Christoph placed his arm around her shoulder.

"Beautiful isn't it? Just like you. You look stunning as usual, by the way."

Salah introduced Rochelle to one of the European dignitaries, Johannes Gottlieb, from Germany. He asked Rochelle about her skating achievements and her travels, and she told him about her desire to become involved in the fight against human trafficking.

"I believe it to be a scourge on civil society. During my travels, I've learned from my many chats how vulnerable people in some parts of the world are being recruited by unscrupulous traffickers with the promise of work in a more affluent country, only to discover, after handing over their hard-earned cash, that they've been duped. Even if they do manage to arrive at their chosen destination, many of them end up in prostitution – a trade I learned so much about recently at the museum in Amsterdam. It's all *so* wrong!" she said, her voice getting higher and louder as she spoke.

"It's a complex and difficult subject – one that's close to my heart, too," Johannes said, recognising her passion about the topic. "There is so much work to be done to identify all the areas of the world, which are at risk of human trafficking, and then to educate the people who live there about what's really going on."

"Do you think there's any training I could do to acquire the necessary skills?" Rochelle asked.

As they chatted, a strange feeling of déjà vu overcame Rochelle, as though she had lived this moment before. For some reason unbeknownst to her, she interpreted it as a sign that this meeting had been destined to happen, and that Johannes was going to be a key player on the route to her new career.

It was as though it was a signal from her parents telling her to trust her instincts. This was the right direction for her. She sensed their presence around her, a connection to them.

CHAPTER 33

Bound for Vienna aboard the final flight of their adventure, Rochelle took out her journal and turned to a fresh page.

She began to write:

What I've Learned During My Journey

There are times when I need to speak up and be heard, but there are also times when I need to keep quiet and listen to what others have to say.

It's fine to push myself out of my comfort zone. Too much self-doubt is not healthy, but some self-doubt pushes me to do better and try harder.

Life is one big learning curve; I will never be too old to learn.

Always remain curious, try to look at things from

other people's perspectives as well as my own.

There will always be occasional bumps on the road of life, but that's all they are. I will always return to level ground.

Believe in myself.

Talent alone does not bring success; hard work and effort pays off in the long term.

Life will give me lots of choices. Whichever path I choose will never be the wrong one; even failures are lessons learned.

Make sure I always make time for the people I love.

Worrying over something won't solve my problems, but taking direct action will.

Always forgive, and try to understand why the person I am forgiving took the action they did.

Speak aloud; never be afraid to voice my opinion as long as my words are said with integrity, and never allow anyone to bully me.

My career and my journey through life are my own, and although I may wish to share it with a partner, my journey will always be mine.

Always be honest to others and also to myself.

Only work in a job that I have a passion for, unless I need money to pay the bills and buy food.

Care about how other people see me, but don't live

by other people's standards, only my own.

Aspire to always do better than I did the day before.

Make every day count, remembering that it may be my last. Never forget Mum, Dad and Lloyd and how their lives were lost when they were young, healthy and strong. Make them all proud of me every single day.

Surround myself with kind, genuine people, and recognise toxic, negative people for who they really are.

Remember that love is more than passion, romance and candles.

Try to help others whenever possible.

Be grateful every day for the small pleasures life has to offer me.

Respect Derek and Gloria for all the love and patience they have given me.

Laugh and sing joyfully at every opportunity.

Try to be sensible with money and always remember the poverty I have witnessed.

Rochelle closed her journal. Out of the blue, she experienced a flashback to the time immediately after her parents' car accident. In that moment, she was back with all of the people who'd helped her in the aftermath: the man who'd rescued her from the twisted wreckage; the squat, redheaded doctor who'd carried her to the ambulance with its flashing blue lights; the kind doctor who'd sat with her and explained about what had happened to her mummy and daddy, at the hospital with the stuffy air and the nasty smell of bleach; the lady with the child in the opposite bed who'd been nice to her; the nurse with the kind face; Amie, the social worker, who'd held her hand in the back of the blue car, all the way to Bristol; and Maddie, her first key worker at the children's home, who'd told her she was a special little girl.

She was shocked at the flow of vivid memories popping into her mind. It was like a jigsaw puzzle piecing itself together. How could she remember them with such crystalline clarity? She'd only been four years old? She suddenly burst into tears, as the memories kept coming.

Christoph leant across the seat and hugged her.

"What's up? Why the tears?"

He handed her his handkerchief.

"It's just old stuff coming back to me. It's dawning on me how lucky I've been, and how grateful I am to have found so much love and care since my parents died. There truly are some good people in the world. You just have to find them … like Derek and Gloria, for instance. I've been shown so much love by them since they took me under their wing."

Christoph's house was set on the edge of a lake. It had an air of rural restfulness, but was close to the small, picturesque town of Hallstatt.

They arrived at sunset, the orange-gold rays stretching across the lake and dipping behind the crest of the mountains on the opposite side of the gleaming water. She stared in awe at the dark-blue lake, which sparkled like crystals. It was one of the most beautiful sunsets Rochelle had ever seen.

"Wow! What a beautiful place," she said.

Pulling her towards him, he kissed her as though for the very first time.

"I planned for us to arrive at sunset. I wanted this to be your first memory of your new home."

The charming house took her by complete surprise.

"It was built in the early 20th century,"

Christoph told her. "My parents renovated it themselves. I hope you're going to like it."

Following him through the front door, Rochelle said, "I love it! It feels like I've arrived in heaven."

He gave her a guided tour, and afterwards poured them both a glass of white wine, which they took outside and sat on the edge of the decking overlooking the lake.

"We'll have to order food in tonight, seeing as we've not had chance to do any shopping … if that's okay with you?" he asked.

"Yeah, perfect. I can't wait to prepare and cook meals for you, though," she said.

"Are you sure it's okay for me to be moving in here with you?"

"Without question, I've been dying to bring you here. My parents would have loved you. They'd so be pleased that you're moving in with me, and I'm not going to be on my own any longer."

"I want to work though, Christoph … earn my own money … do something useful with my life. I'm gonna give Johannes a call sometime this week and see if there's any way he can help me."

"Yeah! I've been thinking about my own career. I still don't know what I'd like to do. I'm looking forward to having Derek and Gloria to stay, though. I want to get to know them better. And I can't wait to introduce you to some of my friends."

The following morning, Rochelle woke bright and early, excited for the next chapter of her life to begin. As she stood sipping a coffee on the decking, she couldn't believe the beauty of her new home.

After breakfast, she and Christoph went for a walk, taking the path along the side of the lake. He enjoyed pointing out some of his favourite places along the way. Rochelle found it one of the most relaxing walks she'd ever taken, and was thrilled at the idea of this being the place she was going to call her home.

Reaching the edge of the town, he led her to an ice cream parlour.

"You can never have too much of the ice cream they sell here," he said.

"There are so many different flavours to choose from, I'm not sure which one to have," Rochelle said.

Christoph smiled at the attractive young

woman behind the counter.

"My usual, please," he said.

She piled the cornet high with Vanilla Toffee Bar Crunch.

"Nice to have you back, Christoph, and sincerest congratulations on the Olympics. It was so amazing to watch."

He put his left arm around Rochelle.

"This is my beautiful girlfriend, Rochelle. Rochelle, meet my lifelong friend, Ariane."

"Oh, my God! You're the ladies gold medallist, Rochelle Erickson."

Rochelle blushed.

"Yeah! That's me. I'll try the Pumpkin Cheesecake flavour, please."

Ariane seemed to pile Rochelle's cornet even higher than she had Christoph's.

"Are you staying long in Hallstatt? Why don't you both come over to mine tonight?"

"We'd love to … if that's okay with you, Rochelle?" Christoph replied.

"Yeah! Wonderful," she replied.

Getting ready to go to Ariane's, Rochelle

was excited at the prospect of spending time with someone who was a close friend of Christoph's.

The tidy, warm house Ariane lived in was smaller than Christoph's, but it had a similar welcoming charm. The drinks and friendly chatter flowed, although Ariane's English wasn't quite as fluent as Christoph's.

Ariane poured Rochelle another large glass of an unfamiliar, but refreshing, white wine.

"It's so beautiful to see two people so much in love with each other," she said. "I've never seen Christoph look so happy. I used to have a crush on him when we were at prep school. But, don't worry, I'm long over him now, and he never did fancy me, anyway."

Rochelle asked a little bashfully.

"Do you have a steady boyfriend, Ariane?"

"No! To be honest, I enjoy flirting too much. None of the men around here take me seriously."

Christoph laughed.

"There are lots who'd show an interest in you, but all you do is tease them."

"I'll let you into a little secret, Rochelle ... actually, Christoph already knows ... if I'm honest, I prefer girls," Ariane said.

"Oh, you should meet my friend, Vanessa. She's the same."

"Vanessa? Not Vanessa Eads, the silver medallist?"

"Yes! That Vanessa. She's my best friend. I'm going to ask her over to stay when she next gets a break from *Disney on Ice*."

"Oh, my God! I'd be beside myself if I met her in the flesh. I really like her."

"Deal done," said Christoph, "Rochelle, let's get her over here as soon as we can."

The evening continued with lots of laughter, Ariane telling jokes and stories from her own and Christoph's school days. Rochelle enjoyed seeing his life from a different perspective, and Ariane's obvious admiration of Christoph touched Rochelle's heart.

Ariane moved to her piano, and she began to play some tunes. Christoph took a place at her side, and Rochelle was shocked by his amazing singing voice … yet another side of him she'd known nothing about.

The following day, Rochelle was surprised to receive a phone call from Johannes.

"Hi, how are you, Rochelle?"

"I'm fine, thank you," she replied.

"I'm phoning because I may have a position available you might be interested in."

Her mind was blown!

"What position?" she asked, excitedly. "Is it something along the lines we were discussing at the hotel in Petra?"

"Yes, I've taken the liberty of setting up an interview for you. It's to be in Salzburg, so not too far from Hallstatt. It would be next Monday at 9am, if you could make it?"

"I've never been to Salzburg, but I'm sure Christoph will be able to get me there."

"This job has your name written all over it, and I've already put in a good word for you."

"That's fantastic. Thank you so much," Rochelle said.

"I'll text you over the details," Johannes said.

"Thank you again. It's daunting, but I'm so excited."

Feeling 12 years old again, Rochelle ran to find Christoph to tell him the good news.

CHAPTER 34

Rochelle sat opposite the female interviewer, who had introduced herself as Zoe Kaufer.

As she explained about the pilot project that had been launched with Salzburg police as part of a European programme, Rochelle focused on maintaining her eye contact as she listened carefully to everything being said. She nodded and smiled at the appropriate times, as Zoe told her that the role would be as a 'victim navigator'.

"Where would the position be located?" Rochelle asked.

"Salzburg, alongside the Salzburg Police Operation Challenger Team. Of course, neutral locations for meetings with victims will also need to be sourced."

"Would I be expected to manage victims

alone, or would that be linked to police procedures?"

"Linked to police procedures, and also to a separate small project steering group. You will need to demonstrate an aptitude for strategic thinking and careful planning."

"So, would it mean I would act independently as a bridge between victims of human trafficking and the police, to help bring criminals to justice?"

"Yes! You would act as an advocate for the victims, helping them to navigate the services they so urgently need."

"Would I need to travel to other countries, too?"

"Yes! You would be expected to visit victims in source countries, who need to remain in contact with the Austrian police, and to assist victims who wish to return to their home country."

An hour later, Rochelle sat with Christoph in a small café near to where the interview had taken place, sipping a cappuccino, whilst he drank his café latte.

"She asked me so many questions, my

head's buzzing. She even asked me which people I most admired in my life, and which personal achievements I was most proud of. I found the whole interview a little emotional. I'm exhausted."

"It's hard to prepare for an interview. You never know what they're going to ask you," Christoph said. "Do they offer much in the way of training? Did you ask about that?"

"Yes! There's a lot of formal training. She said that I came across as pretty self-motivated. We also discussed the support of family and loved ones."

"Well, it's obvious to everyone that you understand the value of persistence and sticking to a task. She'll have recognised that from your skating achievements," Christoph said. "I love you, Rochelle. I'm so proud of you."

"I told her about my adoption, and how lucky I am to have Gloria and Derek in my life."

"You've endured such a lot in your life. She'll have been able to see this, and realise you are an empath," Christoph said.

"She was happy with my exam results, and said it wasn't necessary for me to have a degree because I had other life skills to offer, which were more suited to the role."

"How long did she say it would be before you find out whether you've got the job?"

"About two weeks. They have a few candidates to interview before they make a final decision."

They spent the rest of the day together, with Christoph showing her some of the delights of Salzburg and doing a bit of window-shopping, followed by a relaxing dinner at a cosy Italian restaurant, before driving home to Hallstatt.

The following day, she cleaned the rear, first-floor bedroom, which Christoph had allocated for Derek and Gloria to stay in, and when she'd finished, she placed an ornate vase full of Gloria's favourite flowers on the lacquered bedside cabinet. She was so excited about their imminent arrival. Their flight was due into Salzburg at 4pm.

She turned to Christoph.

"I can't wait to see them. I'm so glad they're coming to stay."

Rochelle spotted them first as they came through the security gate.

"There they are. I can see them," she shouted, excitedly running towards them.

They all hugged one another, and Christoph said, "Welcome to Austria. I hope you're going to like it here."

"Come on! Let's hurry up and get to the car. I can't wait for you to see where we live. You're going to love it," Rochelle said.

Derek laughed.

"Slow down, Rochelle. We've plenty of time. You didn't even ask how the flight was. Well, it was most comfortable, thank you. Got us here in no time."

Gloria grabbed hold of Rochelle's hand and kissed her forehead.

"I've missed you so much. You've no idea."

The week passed by quickly: sailing on the lake in Christoph's little boat; sitting in the old, winged armchairs on the decking, chatting and drinking good Bavarian beer and fruity red wine; eating food like it was going out of style at fancy open-air restaurants; swimming in the lake; visiting the small, but sophisticated, spa with Gloria for a ladies' pamper day; and playing pool at a local, tiny, but well-stocked, bar. Rochelle and Christoph were the perfect hosts, and truly enjoyed entertaining their very special guests.

Although Rochelle shed a few tears at Gloria and Derek's departure back to England, she had never been so happy with her life as she was now. Christoph filled her days with delightful daytrips, showing her the most beautiful parts of Austria. Life was simple, and being in his own native country, he seemed altogether relaxed and happy. It was as though her life had been spattered with a sprinkling of magic dust.

The good news about the job she'd applied for came through quicker than she'd expected. She'd been thrilled to accept their offer, and was looking forward to starting work the following week. She was a little nervous about what lay ahead – the duties she would need to perform, and the responsibilities of the role – but as her first day approached, she became more and more excited at the prospect of fulfilling her dream of helping others in such a rewarding way.

Today, they were spending a day at the beach on the side of the lake. As they arrived, Christoph handed her the key to his little blue and white beach hut.

"Open it up, Rochelle, and put our bags inside."

Rochelle turned the key in the lock and turned on the light, which was powered by a solar panel.

She blinked, almost unable to comprehend the sight before her.

The beach hut was full of flowers, each bloom carrying its own gift tag with a message attached to each one.

She moved to the pink carnations first: *'I will never forget you.'*

Red tulips next: *'I will love you for eternity.'*

Lavender: *'I am devoted to you.'*

Red roses: *'I desire you.'*

Daffodils: *'New beginnings for us.'*

Purple crocuses: *'I want you to be happy.'*

Forget-me-not: *'Never forget me.'*

White clover: *'I'm always thinking of you.'*

Violets: *'I will remain loyal and faithful to you.'*

Red camellias: *'My destiny is in your hands.'*

Sweet peas: *'You fill my life with pleasure.'*

Honeysuckle: *'Our bond will never be broken.'*

She turned to look at Christoph as she moved around the little hut, reading all of the messages over and over.

"How … when did you do this?"

He held a spray of peonies in his hand, and got down on one knee.

"Rochelle, I love you! Will you marry me?"

Tears spilled down her cheeks.

"Yes! Yes! Yes! I will. I love you."

About The Author

S.J.Gibbs is the co-author of *My Rachel* and *The Secrets To Healing With Clear Quartz Crystals.*

The Cutting Edge is her debut novel.

Her short story *Fighting A Battle With Himself* has been published.

She lives in a West Midlands village with her family and two dogs.

Made in the USA
Middletown, DE
23 August 2021